ALIAS JAKE DOLLAR

Chris Morgan was fresh from the army and seeking his old friend, veteran lawman Crossdraw Willard Lester. After Chris saved a tricky character, Jake Dollar, from extermination by outlaw Long Tom Breeze's road agents, Dollar revealed that Lester was dead, murdered — he said — by Breeze's boys. In fact, Dollar himself had killed Lester, hoping to collect the reward offered by the boss of a nearby robbers' roost. Chris coerced Dollar into showing him the way to the robbers' hideout, which proved to be treacherous . . .

Books by Syd Kingston
in the Linford Western Library:

HIDEAWAY HEIST

SYD KINGSTON

ALIAS JAKE DOLLAR

Complete and Unabridged

LINFORD
Leicester

First published in Great Britain in 1974

First Linford Edition
published 2000

British Library CIP Data

Kingston, Syd, *1920 –*
    Alias Jake Dollar.—Large print ed.—
    Linford western library
    1. Western stories
    2. Large type books
    I. Title
    823.9'14 [F]

    ISBN 0–7089–5905–9

Published by
F. A. Thorpe (Publishing)
Anstey, Leicestershire

Set by Words & Graphics Ltd.
Anstey, Leicestershire
Printed and bound in Great Britain by
T. J. International Ltd., Padstow, Cornwall

This book is printed on acid-free paper

1

There was a lot of dust on the trail north of Silver City, in Conchas County, north-eastern New Mexico territory, at nine o'clock on a bright morning in late spring. Many pioneers, merchants and travellers were leaving the town with the prosperous-sounding name after foregathering for a three-day period of festivities to celebrate that time twenty-five years earlier when a lean and somewhat disappointing vein of silver ore had drawn many of the west's regular wanderers to the area in search of easily won riches and a place to settle.

Most of the traffic was headed north, away from the town, but contesting the route in the opposite direction were a few travellers whose business was bringing them south.

Chris Morgan was one of those

riding south against the tide of travellers. In appearance he did not stand out. This was largely because the heat of the sun and the dust of the trail had worked upon him.

A big side-rolled dun stetson had flattened his crisp sandy hair to his head. The steaming long-necked stockingfoot roan masked the length of his long lean body. Although he was still in his twenties, the beginnings of crowsfeet wrinkles were already showing at the outer ends of his clear green eyes. Drops of perspiration glistened in his sideburns. Occasionally, he flapped the brown leather vest which gave extra protection from the weather over his checkered shirt.

Every time a cart or a wagon passed him, the rider examined the crew, but his interest was impersonal. He felt sure that the fellow he was riding to meet was ahead of him in Silver City and that he would be unlikely to leave with those who had merely been to town for the festivities.

Fort Comanche, his last resting place with the U.S. cavalry, was now three days to the north of him. He had opted out after serving for five years and acquiring the stripes of a sergeant. His grading had been good going for a young enlisted man in peace-time with no action to help him on other than occasional isolated skirmishes with roaming Indian gangs.

And now he was free; lured to some extent by the example of one 'Cross-draw' Willard Lester, a federal marshal with whom Chris' company had done useful peace-keeping work at times. Chris now fancied himself more in the role of a peace-keeper, a badge-carrying policeman, rather than a senior army N.C.O. subject to the orders of his superiors.

Whether in fact he could act wisely and well upon his own initiative he intended to find out. Lester, he knew, had a special ambition in this area of New Mexico. He wanted to penetrate the notorious renegades' retreat in the foothills of the Rockies and render it unusable for the future for hit and run road agents and their kind.

Chris wanted to help in this work. By so doing, he hoped to win for himself the confidence of some community and a peace officer's badge. That, and other things. On two or three occasions, Chris had had the pleasure of meeting Nerena Lester, Willie Lester's young female cousin.

Nerena had proved to be as independent and self-reliant as her peace officer cousin. Most of her family were back east, but she found the life there too dull and so she travelled west to where her ancestors had come from. She had shown an abiding interest in the life of the English gentlewoman, Florence Nightingale, and although in America doctors as a rule frowned upon females with medical knowledge and a desire to nurse, Nerena had persuaded two general practitioners to take her on as an assistant.

Consequently, she knew as much

about doctoring as many of the unqualified males following the profession in the western states, and her services were on occasion of great value.

The sudden cracking of a whip over the backs of a sturdy team of cart horses brought the lone rider out of a reverie and back to the trail and its minor irritations. He glanced away to westward, in the direction of the foothills and the towering peaks of the Rocky Mountains further in the distance. The robber's roost was in that direction, and maybe that was the direction of his destiny.

★   ★   ★

Within a half hour, the northward bound traffic began to thin and the willing stockingfoot lengthened its stride, sensing that the journey was almost completed. Chris found himself speculating as to what sort of a reception he would get from old friends after an absence of five years.

He purposely slowed his mount as the first of the buildings loomed up and he concentrated upon first impressions. The end of Main Street was rutted deeper than usual. Mongrel dogs nosed the mounds of horse dirt and screwed up paper and discarded newspapers. The humans in the vicinity moved about with hangdog looks as if the time of the celebrations had taken a lot out of them. Overhead, the cloth streamers which had intimated a welcome to outsiders and explained the nature of the celebrations were in tatters. Here and there were browned-edged holes which suggested bullets fired into the air.

Chris nodded to old acquaintances a couple of times, but he passed by unrecognised and it was clear that the townsfolks' friendliness to visitors had temporarily blown itself out. The rider yawned. After three days of hard-riding in the saddle he had gained his objective. For the first time since he left the army post he admitted to himself that he was tired.

Acting upon impulse, he took the first cross-section out of the main artery, intent upon looking round the other thoroughfares before dismounting and making enquiries about his own prospects and the old lawman he hoped to find.

The heads visible through the windows of offices were scrutinising ledgers and letters. Cafés and coffee houses were busy, but the steam on the windows made observation of the drinkers difficult from outside. The roan snorted a few times as the tour of town dragged on and Chris was wondering which livery to use when a small party outside a saloon on the far side of Second Street took his attention.

He recognised Clint Stocker, the town marshal and his tall, limping deputy, Sam Baron. Stocker was a thick-chested, intense individual with leathery features and brooding brown eyes. His lined face and rounded shoulders made him look his forty years. A red bandanna draped forward accentuated the shoulder weakness and a pinched, weathered one-time dun stetson seemed to boost the size of his features.

Chris coaxed his roan across the street to where they were looking up at the windows and shutters of the drinking saloon, apparently to assess recent damage. Lanky Sam Baron, the deputy, who had just passed his fiftieth birthday, was writing on a paper pad pinned down to a piece of thin board.

Stocker had glanced in Chris' direction without interest and looked away again, but the deputy had recognised him straight away and he paused in his writings. Baron cleared his throat a couple of times, ran his fingers and pencil through his tuft of brown chin beard and over-long sideburns and finally adjusted his black flat-crowned hat, which was permanently upturned at the front.

'This here rider is Chris Morgan,

marshal. The youngster who went away to the army. I figure he wants to speak to you about something important.'

Grudgingly, Marshal Stocker drew his attention away from the damage and the garrulous saloon-keeper who hoped to get some sort of compensation from the town's entertainments committee.

'Yer? Well, howdy, Chris. I suppose we ought to be glad you're back in our midst, but right now we're good an' busy gettin' over the festivities. How come you arrived too late for the celebrations?'

'It's good to see you again, marshal. I couldn't leave in time. The army have a way of hangin' onto you until the very last minute.'

Stocker thought over his reply and shot him a shrewd glance. 'Did you quit the army, Chris?'

'That's right. I quit of my own accord because I wanted to do something different.'

There was a brief silence, while the

roan impatiently shifted its hooves and the peace officers exchanged knowing glances about Chris' earlier ambitions to join the town's peace-keeping force some five years earlier.

Impatient muttering from the saloon owner cut short what might have been a useful and informative exchange of ideas.

Stocker became curt again. 'Was there something you wanted me for, right now, Chris?'

'Not anything that won't keep for an hour or so, Clint. But you could tell me if Willard Lester is in town. I figure you'd know if anyone did.'

Stocker frowned so hard his eyes were almost obscured.

'He means Crossdraw Willie, the federal marshal, I guess,' Baron prompted thoughtfully.

'You serious, Chris?' the marshal queried brusquely.

Chris nodded and waited.

'You think we need a federal marshal of the calibre of Crossdraw Willie to help us keep order in a time of celebration?'

The young rider's expression turned bleak for the first time. He shrugged and smothered a yawn. 'I didn't think anything like that at all. As keeper of law and order I thought you might have seen Lester durin' the last day or two. Now, if you'll answer my question I'll move on an' stop wastin' your time.'

Stocker still seemed annoyed. He was acting as though he wanted an excuse to withold information.

Deputy Baron, stroking down his dark blue shirt, remarked: 'The federal marshal ain't been anywhere near the peace office.'

Chris nodded and thanked him and turned the horse away from the unfriendly trio. He was interpreting the reply as meaning that Crossdraw Willie had not been seen in town. His conversation with the peace officers had left him feeling frustrated. He found himself wishing that he had taken more time over his journey south. There were people he had encountered on his protracted ride who had proved pleasant to converse with and who might have become good friends if he'd spent a little more time with them.

Now, he began to feel lonely. His only close kin, his brother, Bart, was also away in the army. Silver City it seemed, had a short memory for those who had grown up in its midst and the genial camaraderie of the sergeants' mess at Fort Comanche was a thing of the past.

At that stage, he began to think about basic things. First of all, he handed over his horse to a liveryman new to the town and gave no indication as to how long he was staying. Secondly, he had a wash and took a meal in the restaurant of a Chinese who had drifted in from the west coast the previous year.

A full stomach and a few beers made him feel a little better and after that he strolled the boards, once more determined to renew a few old acquaintanceships. An old man cleaning a bar floor admitted to knowing him and presently he approached an old friend of the family, Slim Jenkins, the manager of the Golden Eagle Hotel, a place which must have been more than passing busy in the celebration season.

The nickname 'Slim' was a misnomer for the heavy florid dark-suited man with the thick dark beard and moustache who presided over the best hotel in town.

Chris strolled into the foyer, dismissed the attentions of a bald desk clerk and approached the private office behind the reception as though he had been doing it all his life. The clerk watched long enough and closely enough to be sure that Chris was not some sort of road agent and then he relaxed. Jenkins was minus his jacket and combing his thinning wavy hair with the aid of a mirror mounted on the rear wall.

'The junketin' must have taken it out of you, Slim. I can see a patch of pink scalp through the hair an' that wasn't so when I left!'

The hand which held the comb slowed in its work. Jenkins regarded his visitor's image with half-closed eyes. He then turned about and looked some more as though seeking confirmation. Chris removed his hat to make recognition a bit easier.

Jenkins exploded into a deep fruity laugh and came forward with his hand outstretched.

'Chris! Chris Morgan, in the flesh. Well, this sure is a surprise. I can see the army has managed to fill you out a bit. You were always a mite thin when you used to run errands for me. How've you been? How long are you stayin'?'

Chris shook the hand and thumped the hotelier warmly on the back. In between bouts of laughter and questions he managed to intimate that he was free of the army and at a loose end. He had just explained that he might have to look for work when a waiter in shirt sleeves knocked on the door and stepped inside.

'Mr. Jenkins, we've managed to open the red leather trunk. It contains all the personal belongings of Senator Jim Field, like we thought. But I'm sure we loaded one on to the coach at the same time as the other bags.'

Jenkins was clearly troubled. His face was a mask of anxiety with all the recent joviality completely removed. He patted Chris on the shoulder and stepped past him, crossing the foyer and looking down at an opened trunk. Chris followed him and together they regarded the neatly stacked male clothing with the dark-painted ear trumpet resplendent upon the top.

'That's his, all right. Property of James Field, former senator for the state of Utah. Recently retired. Right now, he's on a fact findin' mission of the western states, an' I'd gamble that foremost in his notes will be the state of existin' hotels and the service he got while makin' his journey! Whatever will he write about *this* hotel when he arrives at Billy Hobday's relay station an' finds his gear is not on the stage? It'll be curtains for us when the word gets around!'

Jenkins was so upset that perspiration had formed on his upper lip. Chris was the one to escort him back to his office and indicate the drawer where he used to keep the liquor bottle, for medicinal purposes. Slowly the manager recovered some of his poise. He located two glasses and poured for the two of them. Chris savoured the whisky, and wondered about his friend's problem. He sat on the edge of a padded upright chair.

'Let me see, Slim, Billy Hobday's place is south of here. Is the coach headed for South Pass, then?'

'That's right. I can't figure how this trunk was left behind. No sirree. By what my boys tell me there must have been another one exactly like it in size an' colour. Somebody pushed this one out of sight behind a settee when we were loadin' up, an' that sure is a darned fool thing to do. What am I goin' to do, Chris?'

'You can't think of anybody who'd ride after the stagecoach with it, Slim?'

Jenkins shook his head rather vigorously. He regarded Chris, then did some more shaking, and finally read his visitor's thoughts. 'Ain't no one at all. Unless you yourself would take on to help me, Chris. I wouldn't ask if it wasn't serious.'

'All right, amigo, I'll take it. You'll have to find me a fresh horse to ride and a pack-horse, too.'

Jenkins gripped him in a bear-like hug. 'Not only that, but I'll pay you as well and fix a room for you when you get back. Are you sure you want to, Chris?'

Although he was quite weary after riding for three days, Chris forced the kind of expression Jenkins wanted to see on his face. Some fifteen minutes later, all preparations were completed. The imposing-looking red leather travelling trunk was strapped to the back of a round-barrelled pinto horse, while Chris mounted up on the back of a black stallion which promised plenty of bottom, although it did not take kindly to the shape of its rider's saddle.

Many speculative eyes followed the rider, the two horses and the pack load down the street. The kind of involvement which Chris had been looking for was not far ahead of him. At this stage, however, he knew nothing of it. He had checked the register of the Golden Eagle for anyone named Lester and had come up with a blank.

He regarded this particular assignment as a matter of no consequence, a makeshift operation to fill in time until fate put him alongside of Crossdraw Willie and evolved a scheme for the penetration of robbers' roost.

2

While Chris was still involved with his friend, the hotelier, a character who was to play an important part in his future was slowly recovering from a recent overdose of whisky in a secluded alcove of a Second Street saloon.

This man, Jake Dollar, by name, had consumed quite rapidly nearly half a bottle of liquor less than an hour earlier. He had drunk with the idea of shutting out of his mind a brief but lethal encounter which had to some extent affected his nerves.

Normally, Dollar would not have recovered his senses so quickly but on this occasion a small injury, almost forgotten in the earlier emergency, pushed him back towards consciousness. Dollar wriggled uneasily on the bench which supported him and cautiously opened one eye to take in his surroundings. On the other side of the room someone was shuffling cards. The barman was mechanically polishing glasses and two men from out of town were arguing about other anniversaries they had attended in western towns.

Everything seemed normal and yet something was making him uneasy. He sat up and studied himself in the wall mirror. He was a tall, lean individual in his middle thirties. His green eyes were slightly aslant, giving him a cunning look which hinted at his true character. He had a wispy line of brown moustache on his upper lip which to some extent minimised the thinness of his face.

He blinked hard, aware of the tiny pink veins showing in the whites of his eyes, and became more conscious of a nagging ache around the back of his neck. At once the mists began to leave his brain and he was back with the scene which he had sought to delete from his mind with the liquor. His struggle to the death with the intensely strong federal lawman, Cross-draw Willie Lester, had lasted less than five minutes, and yet in despatching his victim, Dollar had severely taxed himself.

In order to preserve his identity from spies who would sooner or later have informed about his presence, Lester had entered Silver City by coach, travelling alone and deliberately playing the part of an older man. Dollar was reasonably sure that no one else in Silver City other than himself had discovered the real identity of the short stocky individual who had come from the north ostensibly to take part in the celebrations.

Lester had divested himself of his regular trail clothes and left behind his white stallion which was known to many renegades who feared him. He had grown his greying beard long and he might even have bleached it. His short muscular figure was further disguised in a baggy, grey suit and his long crisp hair was hidden most of the time in a wide flat Quaker style hat.

Among the criminal gangs who operated the southwest at that time, Willard Lester was possibly the lawman most generally feared. Word had come out from the robbers' roost in that county of a guaranteed reward for the elimination of the persistent gang smasher, payable on production of proof to the management of the remote renegades' hideout.

Dollar began to perspire. He shrugged his shoulders without achieving any sort of relief. His dark tailored jacket was a little bit tight across the chest. At this time his brown derby hat appeared to have shrunk a half size. He pushed it back off his sloping forehead and at the same time loosened his black string tie. He was reliving the titanic struggle between the veteran lawman and himself in the confines of the former's room that same morning.

Perspiration beaded his nose afresh.

He knew from earlier observation that Lester partook of an early breakfast and that afterwards he usually retired to his room and smoked a small cigar while reclining upon his bed. He also knew because of information gleaned from a maid at the hotel that the man in room number twelve usually dozed off for a few minutes.

Dollar had been a villain and a known assassin for a number of years. At a time when he had few law-breaking friends inside or outside the robbers' roost he had decided to attempt the biggest 'kill' of the decade to boost his funds and to restore the confidence in him which several notorious gang leaders had once had.

He had entered the room with the aid of a small tool which slipped the badly-fitting lock and was about to knock the still figure unconscious when Lester had shown himself to be very much on the alert. The two antagonists closed with one another at once. There had been no signs of surprise, no protest upon Lester's lips. He had lived with threats upon his life for too long.

Lester could have summoned help by simply shouting out, but was used to making out alone and so he had not shouted. Backwards and forwards the two men had wrestled across the thinly carpeted floor. Dollar was actually getting the worst of the encounter until Lester cracked his head on an iron leg of the bed and temporarily lost the advantage of his phenomenal grip on Dollar's throat.

Seizing his only opportunity, Dollar had contrived to slip his murder weapon — a long-bladed knife — down his sleeve and into his hand. He plunged it rather wildly into Lester's chest and when the older man slowed up and further eased his grip, he withdrew it and rammed it home more accurately into the other's ribs, piercing the heart.

Dollar had backed off thankfully and quickly, anxious to avoid any tell-tale blood. Back on his feet, Dollar had felt an attack of giddiness: more so than he had experienced on other occasions when he had terminated a life.

He now blinked his eyes several times and filled his mouth from the whisky glass still standing on the table beside him. He made a wry face. He had been bold after the event. For a time he had mildly panicked, wondering if anyone was likely to find the dead body in the hotel bedroom. And then, so he had thought, he had a spot of luck. He had noted the red leather trunk. At once he had been struck with its similarity to the one used by the old politician, ex-Senator James Field.

Moreover, he knew from what he had overheard at the hotel dining-tables that the old man from Utah was leaving by coach that same morning.

The exchanging of one leather trunk for another had been slightly nerve-wracking due to the coming and going of members of the hotel staff, but Dollar had achieved his object and switched the tie-on label from one to the other. Consequently, Crossdraw Willie's small compact body, carefully packed in the travelling trunk, had been spirited away by hotel servants and the crew of the stagecoach.

When Dollar had taken on his load of whisky he had thought that his immediate difficulties were over. The coach was bound for South Pass, and the discovery of the body was not likely to take place until the travellers reached Billy Hobday's relay station quite late that same evening.

But now Dollar was not so sure of himself. The nagging ache across the back of his shoulders seemed to needle him back and forth. He reached up to his neck with a nervous hand. It was at that moment he realised to the full his predicament.

His lucky coin, the silver dollar with his name stamped into it, no longer hung there on its slender chain. It had come off in the struggle. Lester must have grabbed it as his clutching hands came off his assailant's neck. *That* was why Dollar's neck ached at the back. The chain had dug into his neck before it had given way under pressure.

More to the point, *where was it now?*

He knew without going back that it was nowhere to be found in the room where Lester had been killed. Very rapidly he came to the right conclusion. There was only one place it could be. In the trunk along with the dead body. The murderer's personal talisman, waiting to be found by doting westerners who treated Crossdraw Willie like a saintly legend in his own time.

That coin with his name on it was a death warrant. There would be such an outcry over the killing that no hideout would be safe to hold him. Outlaws would shun him and others would hunt him. He had blundered very badly, and he knew it; but perhaps all was not lost yet. There was almost half a day before the discovery was likely to be made at the relay station.

The body would have to be recovered, or sent on its travels again to somewhere remote. Even as he thought out his problem, Dollar knew that he would have to open up the trunk for himself. He felt naked without his good luck charm and he would never feel safe if it was left where it was to fall into the hands of strangers. Still feeling very disturbed, but resolute nonetheless, he rose to his feet, paid his dues and strode out into the bright sunlight of noon.

★　★　★

Dollar was able to clear town within ten minutes.

Within an hour his long brown hair was standing out at the nape of his neck and beaded with perspiration. He pushed his big dun horse really hard in an effort to overhaul the South Pass stagecoach with the minimum of delay. His white shirt was sticking to his shoulders. The sudden thought that he would have to mask his face had him dipping in his pockets, searching for a bandanna, an article of clothing which he seldom wore. He found a big red square of cloth bestowed upon him by a dance hall woman in another town. The discovery of it eased his nerves a little.

The winding trail, which skirted the eastern foothills of the Rockies, was a difficult one to negotiate. He rowelled the horse at times and gave it very little respite.

Two hours later, fresh horse droppings warned him that the vehicle was not far ahead. For the first time, he eased his pace and began to think of the coming encounter. He had used the trail before, and now he started to think as the crew of the coach would.

He remembered a small creek often used for the watering of horses. Acting upon impulse, he rode off the trail and made his way through a low patch of scrub, heading for a low mound topped with a screen of low bushes. His off-trail scramble took more than ten minutes. He was breathing as unevenly as the dun by the time it bore him up the last of the slope and brought him out on the useful eminence.

The creek was below him and some

two hundred yards away. Mindful that he could be seen clearly at that distance, he dismounted and pulled out a spyglass which he carried in his saddle pockets. His overheated brow misted up the lens for a time, but he cleared it and excitedly took in the scene which awaited him.

The driver and guard were actually alongside the creek, seeing to the needs of the team of six horses. Further along the waterway, he could identify the full figure of Senator Field in a dark suit and a grey hat with a black band round it. Grouped with the elderly politician were two women and a man who looked like a travelling salesman.

Of greater interest was the red leather trunk which topped the impressive luggage in the coach's boot. He sighed deeply as he saw it and began to think out finally how he would recover control of the trunk. It would be better, he thought, to wait until the team was back in the traces and ready to move on.

The laboured breathing of the dun made him think rather belatedly of its needs. He took off his brown derby hat and poured water into it, offering it to the parched animal. This done, he wiped out the inside of his hat with the red square of cloth before replacing it on his head.

Next, he pulled up a few handfuls of bunch grass and began to roughly groom the animal. Clearly, he could not afford to neglect it as he would need it to put a few useful miles between himself and the coach when he had made his strike. The pressing chores took his mind temporarily off other considerations. He was in the process of slackening the saddle girths when his first intimation of the close presence of others came to him.

Faintly, he heard the sound of horse's harness jingling. He went on with his task wondering if the sound could have carried up from the creek. A second noise made his neck hairs prickle. He ducked under the horse's stomach and came up on the other side, reaching for the twin guns which flanked his slim hips.

As he straightened up, he realised that he was too late to cope with the new threat. On the side away from the trail and the creek several horses were near to him. With his hands on his gun butts he waited tensely. No fewer than three mounted riders came out of the masking scrub at the same time. All of them were aware of his presence. They had their revolvers in their hands.

While he hesitated, and wondered why they were there and looking so militant, two others emerged. The newcomers checked their advance about twenty yards away from him. A deep menacing chuckle came from the lips of the man in the centre, a tall individual with a pointed ginger chin beard and flat deadpan features. He was dressed entirely in black, in contrast to the grey stallion under him.

Dollar recognised him at once. This was Long Tom Breeze, the notorious leader of a group of outlaws who preyed upon outfits in New Mexico, Colorado and Texas. Dollar carefully removed his hands and forced a broad grin of apparent friendliness which he did not feel.

'Boys, you gave me an almighty scare,' he remarked in a low voice. 'I thought at first you were comin' after me. On second thoughts, though, I reckon you must have been movin' in on the coach, as I was. Maybe we ought to talk some before you go into action.'

Dollar was thinking hard. Long Tom Breeze had no special reason to trust him. The Breeze outfit was one of several which regularly made use of the raiders' hideout to westward, and Dollar knew that the word had gone around in there that he was not to be trusted.

Long Tom clicked his tongue. 'I won't put a bullet through your head right now, Jake, but that ain't because I like you. It's because we might alert the coach's crew. So why should the likes of us talk with you before we make our strike?'

Jake shrugged. They were curious about him and that helped a little. He stepped away from the dun towards the crescent of five riders. Long Tom gave a slight nod and two of the riders backed off a little to allow him to approach them in a group.

3

Some thirty yards to the rear of the mound was a natural park bounded by a ring of stones and bushes. The riders retired to this area and Dollar found himself ringed in, along with his horse. Long Tom was slow to make any sort of a move. Instead, he sat his big grey horse and chewed thoughtfully on a split match stick.

Dollar held on to his patience with an effort. He recognised that any quick talking on his part without prompting would be looked upon by Breeze as a sign of weakness. Long Tom's frown grew more pronounced. Eventually, it was one of the gang who broke the silence.

'Shouldn't one of us be keepin' an eye on that outfit down by the creek, Tom?'

Breeze drew his gaze away from Jake

Dollar and blinked owlishly at the man who had spoken. Dollar followed his gaze. He had a feeling he had seen this fellow before, but he could not remember where or when. The rider in question was over the average in height. His hair was very fair and his complexion had a youthful pink glow upon it which denied his thirty-five years. He regarded his leader with troubled blue eyes, all the time fidgeting with his sheepskin vest and the flat-crowned dun stetson which sat squarely above his ears.

'Little brother, you worry too much. You take after your Ma. I wouldn't say the coach is goin' anywhere special, but if you really think we need a lookout why don't we send Ringo? He has good eyes an' his short bandy legs will keep him out of sight an' close to the ground!'

Ringo was about the same age as the younger Breeze, but very different in appearance and outlook. His swarthy complexion and full lined cheeks suggested that one of his parents was a Mexican. A pair of tight-fitting matador-type trousers accentuated the bandiness of his legs and matched the bolero which flapped over his narrow chest.

A broad-faced individual with thick iron-grey sideburns shook with wheezy laughter, but the slightly-built Mexican merely touched his steeple hat and rode out of the group on an equally placid brown-and-white patched pinto.

The younger Breeze remarked: 'Bummer, one of these days Ringo is goin' to take offence when you laugh at him. You ought to go easy!'

Bummer Gorten looked angered. He wanted to retort that Tom had been the one to make the insulting remarks, but he dared not.

'All right, boys, let's light out of leather an' do our talkin'. Take the weight off your legs, Dollar, only keep where we can all see you all the time.'

The note of authority was back in the voice of the outlaw leader and Dollar felt a sort of relief. He squatted down on a flat rock and waited for the others to dismount and arrange themselves around him. As they did so, he studied the fifth member of the gang. This man, who had not spoken, was long-faced, morose-looking. He sported a heavy black moustache which heightened rather than disguised the paleness of his skin. Either his health was indifferent or he was wearing prison pallor. Dollar would have gambled on the latter.

The Breeze gang had only recently moved into Conchas County, and Long Tom's intended strike against the stagecoach had been entirely unpremeditated. He had no idea of the possible contents of the vehicle's strong box or of the identities of any of the passengers. He, therefore, had good reason to try and learn from Dollar.

'So now talk, Jake, if you know what is good for you!'

Dollar brought out a small cigar and casually put a light to it while the lesser mortals in the hostile group waited for their leader's reaction.

'Are you thinkin' of makin' me a temporary member of your gang for this strike, Tom?' Dollar enquired.

'No, I don't have any such intentions. All I want is for you to talk an' talk fast. So why don't you do that an' save yourself a whole lot of unpleasant trouble?'

Dollar blew twin jets of smoke from his nostrils and examined the end of his cigar before complying with Breeze's order.

'Ex-Senator Jim Field is a fairly well-to-do man but he doesn't carry a whole lot of ready money with him on his journeys. I'm interested in him for one item only, his red leather travellin' trunk which you will no doubt have seen perched on top of the boot.'

Dollar stopped talking almost as abruptly as he had started. The faces of young Nate Breeze, Bummer Gorten and the fifth man, Colorado Smith, were bright with speculation. Long Tom stared down at the ground, apparently unmoved, but his brain was working fast.

'This far, Jake, you haven't mentioned the strongbox at all. How come you overlooked it in your explanation?'

'The truth is, I don't know how valuable the contents of the strongbox are likely to be. So why should I lie about it? You're bound to pick up a few hundred dollars, expense money, if you like. Maybe more. Possibly a thousand or two. Who can tell?'

'An' judgin' by your tone, you ain't actually interested. So that means the leather trunk had to be really valuable. I wonder how you found out about that?'

Dollar chuckled. 'I made enquiries about it. Like you're doin' right now, Tom. But why don't we get down to the business in hand? Do I assist at the strike, or do you have other plans?'

A short but difficult silence ended abruptly. 'You don't take part, but there's no reason why you shouldn't stick around.'

Dollar's slanted green eyes half

closed as he glowered at the outlaw leader. 'It's easy to throw your weight around when you outnumber me five to one.' He added quickly. 'All right, but I want you to collect that trunk for me an' let me be the one to open it. Will you agree to that?'

Breeze glowered in his turn, but eventually he made a concession.

'All right, so we won't open the trunk while the coach is still waitin'. Now let's make a move.'

No one needed any second bidding.

★　★　★

Breeze had read Dollar's mind well enough to be assured that he really did want possession of the red leather trunk. That meant that he would not do anything to sabotage the strike against the coach, nor would he make off on his own while the road agents were busy.

Dollar, who was equally shrewd, showed no surprise when he was left behind on the knoll where he had first encountered the Breeze boys. He threw himself down on the warm earth and watched the proceedings from a prone position. The short stop was almost over. The passengers were back in the coach and the driver and guard were in the act of backing the team into the shafts.

While Dollar watched, it occurred to him that he was not seeing the small outlaw, Ringo. He had departed from the observation point before the rest of the gang arrived there. He knew that Ringo's departure had to have something to do with the gang's strategy, so he watched quite closely as the crew finished their chores and mounted up to the box, prior to moving on.

The leading pair of horses were still very frisky in spite of their early efforts. Dollar was massaging his hurt neck and watching them at the same time when he became aware of Long Tom and the three men siding him moving through stunted timber some thirty yards wide of the coach.

There was a narrow sub-stream for them to cross and the observer in the derby hat was beginning to think that they had planned their strike rather clumsily when a sudden shout carried to him from the slight bend in the trail ahead of the vehicle.

'Pull up! Do you hear me? This is a hold-up! Do as you're told an' you won't get hurt!'

Calling out the orders was the slightly built Mexican. His voice sounded more powerful than Dollar would have expected. There was a sudden squealing sound as the brakes were applied in haste.

The driver had sufficient guts to yell a protest. 'Hell an' tarnation! You road agents sure do know when to pick your time! Here we've been stopped for nearly half an hour, an' now you have to show up an' put us further behind schedule! You don't have no consideration for anybody an' that's a fact!'

Ringo ignored his protest. 'Are you goin' to toss that shotgun down into the dirt or do I have to blast you?'

'I ain't sure you could do that, little man!' the guard hurled back belligerently.

At that moment, Long Tom and his three sidekicks splashed through the shallow waters of the lesser stream and revealed their whereabouts to the passengers who were crowding to see through the windows. One of the women gave a cry of alarm. This was sufficient to draw the attention of the crew away from the single mounted man who menaced them to the splashing newcomers.

'You could try to shoot your way out, old timer, but you couldn't eliminate all my friends!'

Ringo sounded confident and he was right. Grudgingly the bearded guard dropped his burnished shotgun and told the passengers over his shoulder that they were in trouble.

Within two minutes the stationary coach was ringed by the five riders. The angry senator needed little persuading to remove himself from the interior and presently the salesman and the two women followed him down to trail level, peering apprehensively this way and that. Clearly, they had little experience of seeing mounted men with masked faces and they were very frightened.

'All right, ladies, there's no real cause for worry. Jest so long as you do as you're told. Now, kindly line up with the two gents an' produce your valuables when my man moves along the line.'

The voice was that of Long Tom and he sounded almost amiable with his ginger beard hidden behind a bright yellow bandanna. His brother, Nate, was the one to slip out of leather and hold out his stetson to receive the offerings.

The salesman was muttering heatedly to himself. The purport of his words indicated that he had been robbed in a similar fashion on two previous occasions and the thing was beginning to be a habit. He handed over a small leather purse with two eagles in it and a few lesser coins.

Jim Field was determined to exchange words with the young ruffian with the full head of sun-bleached corn-coloured hair. He blustered, while he toyed with his gold hunter watch and a fistful of double eagles which he kept in his waistcoat pocket.

'Tell me, young fellow, what sort of an upbringin' did you have that forced you to take up stage robbery at your age?'

'We was passin' poor, mister, passin' poor. We often do this, but we don't feel any sort of guilt, an' that's a fact. So why don't you make a mental note of that an' send it to congress or something?'

Field coughed with amazement, realising that this rawboned young fellow actually knew who he was. He was still blinking with surprise when the spinster sisters gave over their savings which had been hidden in their voluminous skirts, secreted in soft embroidered purses.

'All right, now, folks, you can get back into the coach. Our personal business with you is concluded.' Tom turned his attention to the crew, who were waiting apprehensively and wondering if they would have to contribute to the raiders' collection from their own pockets. 'You two up there, toss down the strongbox, an' be really careful. As soon as you've done that, I want you to move around to the boot and wait for further instructions!'

At first, driver and guard were slow to comply, but when Ringo and then Colorado prompted them with a display of impatience and shooting irons, they rose from the seat and lugged out the heavy box from under it. A cloud of dust rose from the trail near the rearmost horses as the metal box landed with a dull thud.

Dollar, distantly placed, rose to his feet and watched intently at full stretch while Bummer and Nate Breeze lugged the box further away and blasted the three locks off it with casual revolver shots. One horse reared up and tugged away with fear. Three others showed similar signs and the air was filled with frightened snickering.

Three large rocks accounted for a lot of the weight in the treasure box, but there were two leather satchels in with them and between them they contained almost a thousand dollars in notes and coins. Directly after the box was emptied, the crew went to the rear and the magnificent red leather trunk was lowered to the trail with great care.

Standing on the top of a rock, Dollar watched and perspired. He reflected that it was almost as if the crew knew the contents, so much respect were they showing for the article. On the top of the mound, James Field's long and eloquent protests were muted by distance.

There were two minutes which followed when Dollar thought Long Tom was not going to be able to resist the temptation to open it on the spot: but the emergency passed, and Nate Breeze — with a great effort — man-handled the trunk across the back of his mount and clumsily forked the horse behind it.

Some six or eight bullets blasted skywards helped the coach and its contents upon its way to the relay station, and within a couple of minutes the sounds it made faded from the ears of the raiders. Dollar mounted his dun and came down off the mound to join the others.

He had no questions to ask as to which direction they intended to take. He was certain that Nate had with him the same red trunk which had been loaded aboard the stage by mistake. He was back in the presence of the late Crossdraw Lester. That meant that the evidence could be removed from the trunk which this far had been used like a coffin. But was this the best time to open the trunk and reveal to these hostile outlaws that there was no treasure as such inside it at all?

Dollar doubted it very much and he left the immediate future to fate. Nate swung to a halt not far from him, and the weight of the trunk made him lower it to the ground.

'Are we goin' to take a look at Dollar's private treasure, big brother, while we have the chance?'

Long Tom, who was dabbing perspiration out of his beard with the yellow bandanna, hesitated. He glanced at Dollar, who shook his head.

'All right, so we make tracks further west, I guess. But you don't have to carry the trunk. Let Jake take it up on that dun with him. After all, it is supposed to be more than passin' valuable.'

Dollar complied with the instructions, showing no enthusiasm.

4

Chris Morgan, mounted on the borrowed black stallion, left Silver City within half an hour of Jake Dollar's departure. He found that the black was in good fettle and capable of putting up a fine time on the way to the relay station, but unfortunately the pinto which had to tote along the invaluable red leather trunk did not have such an easy task.

The trunk was a bulky article and from time to time it slipped to one side in spite of the careful knotting of the lariat which held it in place. Consequently, Chris did not keep up with Dollar's rate of progress and that was why the hold-up of the coach had happened and gone into the past before he reached the spot on the trail where the clash had occurred.

Chris had an idea of the estimated

time of the stage-coach's arrival at the relay station, and so, in the early hours of the evening he reduced the speed and effort of his two horses, giving them an easier time. He was content to arrive at the isolated settlement within an hour of the vehicle.

It was around seven o'clock when the two horses, looking quite a bit the worse for their efforts, started to approach the tidily-kept buildings and corral which were the property of Billy Hobday, a Civil War veteran with a rare sense of humour and a wooden leg from the left knee downwards.

The relay man himself, a veteran of sixty years was crossing the paddock with a bucket in his hand when Chris started to approach. He put down the bucket and pivoted upon the tip of his wooden leg as he studied the newcomer and the load carried by the pack horse. He whistled and called to his son, Gunter, who had lived all his twenty-three years on the station.

'Son, will you take a look at this

hombre an' tell me if his face is familiar? Then take another look at that red trunk an' tell me if it sounds like the one stolen by the outlaws!'

Chris knew Billy Hobday, having seen him on countless occasions before he — Chris — joined the army. In fact, Billy had been one of those to encourage the Morgan boys to join up in the cavalry. Chris did not expect that Billy would still recognise him, however, and he was in for a pleasant surprise.

The old man in the denim overalls and shapeless broad-brimmed hat was showing every sign of having recognised him. He was gripping his crisp wavy white beard and the bright eyes under the tufted grey brows were alive with interest.

Gunter Hobday was a much younger version of his father. He was better off, having the use of both limbs and he kept his face clear of hair by daily shaving. Gunter raised his straw hat and slowly grinned.

'This sure is a day full of excitement, Pa. That there is the young hombre who went off to the army five years ago. Name of Chris Morgan, an' that red trunk surely has to be the one the senator is eternally complainin' about!'

Chris was near enough to have heard some of the exchanges. He dismounted quickly by the gate which the young Hobday opened for him and contained his patience long enough to exchange warm greetings with the keepers of the place before making his own enquiries and giving explanations.

Gunter took away the two horses and Billy led Chris to the rear of the establishment to show him to his two sisters who helped to run the place. Chris kept the introductions short, on account of his unkempt appearance and his burning curiosity.

It was while he was under the pump that he heard much of the exciting news about the stage being held up on the way from Silver City. Billy's description enabled Chris to pin down the location of the hold-up while he was still breathing hard under the cool water.

He risked swallowing a lot of water when he asked for an explanation about the red leather trunk which was stolen at the hold-up. Billy did not know the answer and that part of the revelation had to remain a mystery.

While Chris finished his ablutions, old Billy rambled on and the ex-army sergeant learned a whole lot more before he was finally led indoors to meet the travellers.

Senator Field had talked loudly almost the whole of the rest of the journey after the hold-up. On arrival at the station, the two ladies had retired for a while to recuperate from his heavy dialogue. The brief exchanges with the outlaw at the hold-up had not been affected by his deafness because both he and Nate Breeze and been talking loudly on account of the excitement of the occasion and their being out of doors.

Subsequently, however, he had increased the volume of his voice and the ladies had been hard put to it to make him hear at all, his ear trumpet not being available.

In the dining-room, the delighted senator had his trunk open and he was posturing in front of the other guests, putting his ornate ear trumpet into first one ear and then the other. Billy announced Chris as the young fellow who had brought the trunk from Silver City and Field took over from him. The ladies moved around him, and even the salesman, who preferred more flashy, worldly company, showed more than a passing interest.

The men drank whisky and the women sipped wine. Ten minutes later, the Hobday women ushered them to the table and put the first course in front of them. Jim Field said a brief grace, nodded easily to the others and at once resumed his conversation with Chris.

As the trumpet wagged towards him,

the sandy-haired young man grinned over his soup and explained. 'There had to be two trunks back there in Silver City, sir, which were almost identical. Obviously, the wrong one was loaded. Now that I have learned that the other one was deliberately stolen by road agents I must admit to being very curious as to its contents.'

Chris was hungry. The contents of the stolen trunk remained uppermost in his mind, but he listened politely to all the travellers in turn and did his best to satisfy their curiosity as to his re-appearance in the county and his recent manoeuvring.

Shadows were creeping across the low beams of the sitting-room and the ladies had long since retired when Chris, for the first time, began to ask some questions on his own account. He explained how he had come to Silver City with the express intention of contacting an old friend, who had proved very elusive.

'What makes the matter even more

difficult is that my friend might well have disguised himself in an attempt to keep his identity a secret.'

Field weighed up these revelations and snorted over his tobacco pipe. Eventually he coughed and winked in a conspiratorial fashion at the salesman sitting opposite.

'Well, young fellow, you've done me quite a service today, so why don't you describe your friend's appearance an' I'll try an' figure out if I ran across him durin' the celebrations.'

The other listener nodded encouragingly, and Chris began.

'My friend could not disguise his size very well. He is short, stocky and muscular. Usually, he wears a fairly full beard. It was greyin' a lot the last time I saw him. His hair is long on the top of his head and his brows are curling and jet black.'

'Say no more,' Field boomed, but the salesman, who had also fitted the description to somebody, butted in.

'I'd bet a dollar to a plugged nickel

that's the old professor. The one with the Quaker hat and grey suit! I thought he was still in the hotel when we left.'

Field nodded very decidedly. 'He was no professor because I challenged him about the college he claimed he came from, somewhere in Kansas an' he changed his story. But he could have been your friend, on account of his build an' his explanation not hangin' together.'

There was a short argument between Field and the other man, but at the end of it they were fairly certain that the traveller in question had called himself Professor George Wills, and that he claimed to be from Wichita, in Kansas. Chris was so excited that he went looking for Billy although the hour was late. Young Hobday had the ability to send messages in morse, and the station was actually on a telegraph line.

Gunter roused up without enthusiasm when told what he must do. He read over Chris's message two or three times and slowly began to work the morse tapper. His speed was phenomenally slow and his spelling was not too good, but eventually he managed the whole message and received back a signal from Silver City saying that the message had been understood and that a reply would be put through in due course.

Some forty minutes later, the reply came. Gunter wrote it down with a blunt pencil while Chris, Billy and James Field stared over his shoulder.

Professor George Wills has not been seen about town all day. Clothes still in his room. It is thought that he is still about town somewhere. Message ends.

The four men walked out on to the gallery at the rear of the main building. Chris was slow to make any comment on the message, and the senator had to press him for his views.

'All I can say, gents, is that my friend was on a special hush-hush assignment, and that he may have run into trouble. I shall have to get back to town early tomorrow to look into the matter.'

Shortly after that, they all turned in.

★   ★   ★

Chris ate his breakfast before the passengers reached the table, and he was anxious to be on his way when they trooped out to say their farewells to him. He rode the black stallion hard, so that the pinto which had borne the red leather trunk had difficulty in keeping up.

Covered in dust and perspiration, and feeling despondent about Cross-draw Willie, the young ex-cavalryman entered the town in the middle of the afternoon. He made straight for the Golden Eagle Hotel and had a talk with Slim Jenkins. Together, they examined the room which the elusive professor had occupied. All his spare clothes were in evidence, but there was no sign of weapons, or of a suitable valise or trunk in which to pack his gear.

Feeling more depressed than ever, Chris took a glass of wine with Jenkins, answered a few questions about the hold-up on the way to South Pass, and excused himself rather bluntly in order to make his own search of the town.

Already he was getting round to the idea that the extra red trunk might have been the property of Willie Lester, but this far he had no sort of inkling of the contents. Within an hour, he had visited all the obvious places and learned nothing.

He was walking down Second Street with his shoulders hunched when he spied the shingle of the local doctor. The surgery was closed, but Doctor McCann admitted him to his sitting-room without demur, as he had heard of Chris' exploit and the coach hold-up.

Automatically, the young man answered while he sipped a glass of lukewarm beer. He then described Professor Wills, and watched the veteran doctor's jutting brows rise above his eroded eyes.

'Glory be, young fellow, the man you describe came to see me at the beginning of the festivities. He had nothing wrong with him, but he was enquiring about a young woman named Nerena Lester!'

At the mention of Nerena's name, Chris stiffened on the edge of his upright chair. He put down his glass on the grey velvet table cloth and leaned forward, his green eyes at first rounding with surprise and then showing a remarkable intentness.

'And were you able to give him any information, Doc?'

The older man nodded, massaging his white sideburns and studying his visitor's face.

'Sure, Nerena Lester, a very present-able young woman, came to Silver City a couple of months ago. She wanted to work for me, but I put her off at first. Then there was an accident to a family comin' in by conestoga. She got there early on. It was clear by the way she performed that she knew as much about medicine as many men in these parts. So I gave her a job, and she worked well for two or three weeks.'

The doctor's voice had slowed and his gaze became distant.

'And then she moved on again?' Chris prompted.

'She moved on quite suddenly without warnin' and without supplyin' a particularly good excuse. I was more than passin' annoyed at the time. You see, I had the impression that she was so keen on doctorin' that she would not have moved on except if she had a better job than I could offer her.'

Chris nodded suddenly. 'I think you're right in your assessment of her attitude. Since she quit workin' for you, though, nothin's been heard of her?'

McCann confirmed that Nerena had not been back. He talked on, giving details as to how she had handled patients and how she had endeared herself to many of the townsfolk in just that short time.

Chris asked other questions, but he became no wiser. Five minutes later, he stood up, thanked the doctor for the drink and shook hands with him. Out of doors, the young man slowed up in the heat of the afternoon. He was scowling when he presented himself at the office of the town marshal and reflecting to himself that Silver City was a town of mystery as far as he was concerned.

Crossdraw Willie had disappeared from it, and now it was clear that Nerena had paid a visit and also withdrawn without leaving a forwarding address. Chris thought that he would have to become a detective of sorts before he could link up with his friends and share in their future plans.

Marshal Stocker offered him a chair which was more rocky on its legs than that of the doctor. The peace officer was still a bit cool towards Chris, but he seemed a little more friendly than on the occasion of their previous meeting. Sam Baron, the deputy, was elsewhere and as Stocker had to keep awake in the office, he decided that nothing was to be lost by chatting with the somewhat intense ex-soldier.

He offered him a small cigar, which was accepted.

'I hear you missed out on a bit of excitement yesterday. Tell me, though, did you find Crossdraw Willie on your travels?'

'Nope. Not this far, Clint. But I think he was in town over the festivities, stayin' at the hotel. I can't understand what's happened to him. Somehow, I figure Willie's trunk got itself aboard the South Pass coach, but Willie himself has vanished. I don't have any idea where he can have got to. Nor does anyone else in town. One thing is for sure. He has enemies. What's more, I'm convinced there are men in this town who wouldn't hesitate to take messages to the robbers' roost for a few dollars.'

'You think Willie was plannin' some sort of a raid on the robbers' roost?'

Chris nodded. 'It was always in the

back of his mind. That's why I'm bothered about him right now. If he could enter Silver City an' remain unrecognised during the festivities, other men might have done the same thing.'

There was a short, awkward silence between the two men. It was finally broken by the town marshal.

'Well, Chris, I don't rightly know what your plans are from here on in, but you can count on me for help, if you need it. Is there anything I can do right now?'

Chris grinned briefly. 'There's one thing I'd like you to do for me, Clint. Turn out the drawer with the reward notices in. I'd like to take a look at the faces. Maybe you'd look with me, because you must have seen a lot more profiles of strangers recently than I have. After all, I was a late arrival.'

Stocker bristled a bit inwardly, feeling that young Morgan's probing might throw some doubt upon his own efficient handling of the town, but he controlled his immediate reaction and complied with the request. Most of the notices were yellowing and dog-eared and quite a quantity of dust came out with them.

Many of the faces were familiar to Stocker. He blinked and nodded, becoming more and more confident that none of them had been in his town in the past few days. Chris reached out for one which was near the bottom of the pile, and which Stocker was about to turn over without comment.

Chris' action drew them together, and they both studied the unusual features of the crafty, lean-faced individual with the slightly slanted eyes. Stocker scanned the wording with his eyes half-closed.

'Jack Doolin, alias James Delonge, alias Jake Dollar. I have to admit that I caught a glimpse of a face like that not long ago. Wanted for armed robbery in four counties of three states and territories. What's this pencilled on the bottom? One time bounty hunter turned assassin. Uses gun and knife, mostly.'

Stocker left the notices on his desk and followed Chris out into the open. As they entered the hotel, the marshal was muttering to himself, 'Uses a gun and a knife, mostly . . . '

★ ★ ★

Dollar had gone without trace, of course, but Chris thought his sudden withdrawal at the time of Willie Lester's disappearance was likely to be more than coincidental. A liveryman knew the approximate time when Dollar had withdrawn his dun from the stable.

5

Chris availed himself of the room put at his disposal by his friend, Slim Jenkins. After stripping down and getting under the pump in the rear yard of the hotel he went to his bed and stretched out upon it. Sleep eluded him for a while, but presently he slipped off into unconsciousness although his mind was troubled.

Two hours later, he rose, dressed himself and took a meal in the hotel dining-room. After that, he went out on the town, taking a drink here and there, checking and double-checking with various people who now seemed better disposed towards him that the diminutive professor was nowhere about.

Jenkins rose early the following morning in order to have a chat with him over breakfast. Chris had intimated the night before that he intended to leave town and explore the terrain towards South Pass in a protracted search for his friend, for Jake Dollar and for the missing duplicated red trunk. He had a feeling that there was some sort of a link-up between the two men and the trunk, and while he was worried about Willie he could not settle in town.

Jenkins stood by the stockingfoot's head with his hands on his hips, peering up at Chris who was sitting his saddle rather restlessly.

'You'll let us know of any developments, Chris?'

'Sure, I'll be glad to do that, Slim, although I must admit I don't like the indications so far. In the event of Willie turnin' up, or his cousin, Nerena, be sure to tell them where I can be located.'

The two shook hands briefly. Chris rode off without looking back and Jenkins went slowly up the street, shaking his head in doubt and wondering what the outcome of his friend's investigating would be.

In an isolated spot, well clear of the area where a sheriff's posse was belatedly looking for the road agents, Long Tom Breeze's gang went to earth and slept easily, undisturbed by anyone.

Every member of the gang with the exception of Long Tom was burning with curiosity about the contents of the trunk. Long Tom himself was surprised to find that Dollar was prepared to turn in and sleep without opening the trunk. He knew that he was in a position to force Dollar to open the article, or have it opened without his consent. But he did not press the matter until the following morning.

Bummer prepared the breakfast which consisted mostly of bacon and biscuits washed down by coffee. It was when they had all eaten their fill and were smoking cigarettes and cigars that the gang leader's curiosity got the better of him.

A silence fell upon the lounging group, during which the leader's speculative gaze never left Dollar's face. The latter developed a slight twitch in one cheek and without saying anything he was prepared for the revelation which had to come. 'Do you want me to open the trunk myself,' he questioned, at last, 'or would you prefer to do it yourself?'

A current of excitement engulfed the other members of the gang. Tom grinned slowly without removing his stogie from his lips.

'You do it, Jake,' he instructed casually. 'But no tricks, huh?'

Dollar stood up and dusted down his trousers and jacket which had lost some of their smartness due to sleeping on the rough earth. He eyed them all keenly, and produced a small key from his pocket with a flourish not unlike that which a conjurer might have used. Next, he knelt beside the trunk and undid the holding lock. This, he threw on the ground. The lid was back in an instant and the others crowded him close to see the contents.

There were gasps of surprise and one or two rounded oaths as the slightly crumpled figure of the small bearded man in the baggy clothes was revealed to them.

'What in tarnation is this, Jake? You tryin' to make a fool of us, or something?' Nate Breeze protested.

Dollar shook his head, but did not explain straight away.

'You led us to believe that there was treasure in the trunk,' Smith pointed out, 'an' now you show us this. A small dead man an' nothin' else in there but a weapon or two!'

Dollar shrugged, and Breeze's minions turned to him, expecting him to take charge of the puzzling performance. Long Tom fingered the ginger tuft on his chin and eyed Dollar speculatively.

'If you've got a fortune buried under that small corpse, Jake, now is the time to make your explanation. Show it to us!'

'There's no extra loot in the trunk,

Tom, other than one small item which clearly belongs to me.'

Dollar pushed Ringo and Bummer aside and collected from the clutching hand of the deceased his broken chain with the dollar attached to it. He held it up for all to see, and showed them the rear side with his name stamped into it.

'There, you see? My good luck token. A silver dollar. It has my name on the back of it. I wear it all the time!'

The expression on Nate Breeze's face grew ugly. 'Are you tellin' us you had us lug this trunk all the way here simply because you'd lost your good luck charm? Is that what all the mystery is about?'

Dollar adjusted his derby hat and looked away into the distance. He knew how angry the gang were and that they would continue to be that way for a time. He felt that his revelations, given in a calm fashion, however, would ride him over the worst of their vicious reactions.

Ringo and Bummer, following a nod

from Long Tom, raised the stiff corpse with some difficulty and laid it on the ground beside the trunk. Two or three minutes were sufficient to show that nothing of a valuable nature was hidden in the article.

Suddenly, the attitude of the frustrated outlaws changed. Four of them crowded the unpopular loner, waiting for an order from their chief. Dollar blinked hard, thinking this was the time for revelations, but Long Tom's signal took him by surprise.

Nate hit him hard on the side of the jaw, knocking him off balance and sending him towards Ringo and Bummer. The small Mexican deftly lifted Dollar's guns out of the holsters before Gorten hit him in the back and sent him sprawling again. Breathing hard, Dollar teetered between the four of them, taking their punches and gradually losing his breath.

His temper flared for an instant and he lashed out at Colorado Smith, but the moustached man was fitter than his prison pallor would have led anyone to believe. He grabbed the arm which swung at him and held on. His expression changed as he felt the long-bladed knife strapped to the forearm.

Smith clicked his tongue. Ringo stepped forward to help him and between them they removed the sharp weapon and at the same time checked the rest of his clothing for other weapons. This time they found nothing. Dust rose in the small arena as the fists went in and nearly five minutes elapsed before Dollar sank to his knees and gasped out his breath, following a kick in the side from a pointed riding boot toe.

'All right, boys, that's enough for now,' Long Tom remarked considerately.

The quartette reluctantly backed off and rubbed themselves down, having suffered in the heat. They settled back a yard or two, making roughly a square around their prisoner, who was in no hurry to show further defiance and thus risk a further beating.

Long Tom himself looked over the corpse and quickly ascertained the mode of death. He picked up Dollar's knife and balanced it delicately in his hand. Then he started to toss it from one hand to the other. He did not look at his hands as he did this, and something in his manner prompted Dollar to speak.

'I'm disappointed you didn't recognise the corpse,' he murmured, through cracked lips.

For a time, no one spoke. 'So who is he?' Nate queried grudgingly, after an interval.

'He's Willard Lester, one of the best known federal officers in the west,' Dollar explained, with conviction.

Nate laughed off-key. 'You're tellin' us that's Crossdraw Lester an' that you despatched him with that knife? You're makin' it up, amigo! Lester has a reputation for sleepin' with one eye open!'

'I don't deny that, Nate. In fact you can see he has his eyes open now, in death!'

Smith aimed a feinted kick at Dollar, hoping to stir further revelations out of him, but the man on the ground merely rolled sideways and remained wary.

Ringo remarked: 'This corpse is the right sort of age for Lester, Tom.'

'An' he has his holsters slung on his hips like a crossdraw gunman would have,' Gorten added evenly.

'So what if he *is* Crossdraw Lester, an' he's dead by your hand?' Long Tom probed. 'Where do we go from here?'

Dollar raised his right hand and pointed his index finger at the leader. 'You'll allow you've only jest arrived in this territory from the north. If you'd been operatin' these parts lately you'd have known that there's a price on Lester's head, put there by the Boss of the hideaway! Everybody knows the Colonel thinks he's a menace, so I've removed him an' I aim to collect the reward for him! Don't that make sense?'

'It does if you can get into the hideaway unmolested, Jake,' Tom conceded. 'Only we heard you weren't popular out there any more. Too many groups have been sayin' that you don't share fairly with your pardners. The word has gone around. You might have done a risky killin' for nothing — if this really *is* Willie Lester!'

Dollar suddenly rose up on his knees, waving his arms and making a plea. 'Will you give me a chance to look over the body an' the other things, Tom? I feel sure I can prove to you that this is the right hombre! Let me take a look, will you? You have nothin' to lose right now!'

Long Tom tinkered with and split a match stick with Dollar's murder weapon, but eventually he gave the required permission. Dollar sprang forward and began to go over every item of clothing. Those around him knew what it felt like to be under pressure and they never desisted from mocking him and talking about what his imminent and premature end ought to be.

Dollar was as surprised as anyone else when he found the tarnished federal marshal's badge in the bottom of a soft black leather boot. He held it up in triumph for all to see, breathing hard like a landed fish all the time. He tossed the badge to Long Tom who caught it and examined it non-committally and tried it on the front of his shirt.

'If this is Crossdraw Willie, I don't believe you killed him for a reward which you might not live to collect. I think you killed him for the money he had with him. How does that sound to your cunning ears, amigo?'

'I never did have the time to search him properly, on account of he was in a hotel, in daylight, when I jumped him. You can search me if you think I took a big wad from him!'

The quartette promptly took him at

his word and rolled him and searched him from head to foot. They seemed disappointed when he only had on him one roll of folding money amounting to less than one man's share of the coach loot.

Long Tom shook his head, but did not appear disappointed.

'He's a crafty one, this Jake. He wouldn't have a whole lot of money on him where we could find it. But if we kept him hobbled for a few hours, he might have a rush of memory and tell us where to look for a few thousand dollars. In the past, the jaspers who have worked with him didn't take him seriously enough. I reckon if we pegged him out in this dry soil an' left him here with the corpse for company he'd be more than keen to tell us anything we wanted to know in a few hours. What do you say, little brother?'

Some of the stiffness went out of Nate's face. 'You think maybe when the vultures come around he'd appreciate our company, Tom?'

The leader nodded. Once again, the outlaws grabbed Dollar and held him firmly. This time they tied rope to his arms and legs and pinned him out in the dry soil, using shackling pins. Acting in unison, they began to withdraw.

Tom was the one to come back and gag Dollar with his red square of cloth. Almost as an afterthought, the gang leader threw a blanket over the corpse. This last gesture offered Dollar no relief. He knew that carrion birds could smell out death over large distances. Dollar turned his head to watch the withdrawal. In doing so, he lost his hat.

★   ★   ★

A good quarter of a mile away: out of sight and sound, the outfit pulled up. The others wondered what was in Long Tom's mind. He quickly put them at ease.

'I think Jake has been levellin' with us this trip, boys. But he may know the whereabouts of a whole lot of buried loot. So, I figure we go back to him in a few hours' time an' shoot some bullets close to him an' see what effect that has on his forked tongue.'

Smith chuckled first, and soon the others had joined in. This was the sort of humour they could understand and appreciate.

6

The stockingfoot roan was well rested for that exacting day's ride and consequently Chris pushed it hard until he was within a mile or two of the spot where the coach had been robbed. After that, he allowed it to walk and the spot he used for freshening up was the same one which the coach's crew had selected for their horses.

While he lay prone at the water's edge slopping water over his head and neck, he tried to put himself into the thoughts of a capable outlaw leader who wanted to withdraw to a safe distance in a big hurry. Not much thought was needed to arrive at the conclusion that the north was not a likely direction.

The gang could have ridden east and risked tangling with the county sheriff's riders, but only if they were intent upon crossing the border with Texas. Chris was doubtful about that direction, too. So it had to be south or west.

In a southerly direction there was little to commend itself to men riding away from the threat of a posse, and to westward civilisation ran out in about two day's ride. On clear days, the easterly line of foothills which marked the beginning of the Rockies was clearly visible, and some distance behind them the nearer bulking pinnacles of the mountain range appeared to hang in the sky like a highly-coloured back-cloth.

Westward was the outlaw's traditional direction of withdrawal, at least in that county. No one who had not been there knew the exact dimensions of the robbers' retreat hidden on the near side of the peaks, and the few who knew would not risk their necks by giving away the secrets.

All this Chris knew before he finally stood up, remounted and moved on again. He felt almost certain that the successful road agents would have withdrawn nearer to the rockies because that was the way of safety for them.

Consequently, as he came away from the stream he found himself heading almost due west and proceeding with some confidence. Within three miles, the firm terrain gave way to undulations which put some small strain upon horse and rider.

It was an area which had suffered some thousands of years ago when the earth's crust had been distorted by heat from within. Low ridges and shallow valleys furrowed the earth this way and that, sometimes clothed with scrub and bunch grass and at other times bare, or dotted with occasional cactuses and dwarf trees.

Chris pressed on for another hour and then he reined in on the top of a mound which was ringed by stunted oak trees. While the roan shifted its hooves restlessly, he extended his spyglass and curiously put it to his eye.

For a minute or so, he forgot the group of riders who were his immediate quarry while he feasted his eyes on the distant vistas brought closer by the lenses. The upper slopes of the Rockies were clothed in many colours even at that time of the day, and the nearer buttes and mesas seemed indistinct by comparison.

He knew from his earlier explorations, carried out before he joined the army, that the immediate surroundings of the robbers' roost were ill-defined on maps. They were a mixture of dry gorges, running and still creeks, gnarled rocky outcrops and puzzling remote canyons. The rocky character of the region was very old, but some of the lush green verdure which liberally dressed the lower foothills reminded the lone rider of the recent spring and nature's reawakening.

As he gazed, with one eye closed and the other very near to the spyglass lens his ears were attuned to the noises of nature. He picked out the differing squawks and cries of birds and detected the sounds of small wild animals in communication with each other.

Nothing happened to disturb his composure or his speculation until a large turkey-buzzard glided across the sky in front of him, moving from north to south, silently intent upon something hidden from the human eye.

He lowered his glass and watched it through half closed eyes as it altered direction and finally dipped lower, to disappear from view behind a distant line of trees which resembled a green cockerel's crest. What had drawn the bird of prey in that direction? he wondered.

His shoulders drooped. He felt suddenly tired. He made his further observations from a standing position, seeing nothing at all which suggested that he had come near to other humans. Once again, the vastness of the region in which he had grown up impinged upon his senses.

He found himself wondering at his

own brand of optimism which had led him to search for a group of men as wild as the animals of the region and as adept at keeping out of sight. He knew that he would have to have phenomenal luck to locate the road agents and that any future contact with Willie Lester and the other man he sought would border on the miraculous.

He found himself yawning, and, as his spirits were at a low ebb, he decided to take a rest. He slackened the saddle, gave the roan a drink and finally stretched himself out on his back with his stetson shading his face. Within minutes, he had slipped into a light daytime sleep.

★   ★   ★

The staccato gun shots roused him quite suddenly and gave him a feeling of guilt over his sleeping. He sprang to his feet, looked around for the spyglass and at once applied it to his eye.

Undulations to the south masked the

scene of the action from him, but his ears told him that several guns, probably revolvers, were being fired off by a number of men. Now and then he thought he heard shouts, but he could have been mistaken.

His first inclination was to mount up and ride nearer. He obeyed his instincts with his mind busy and came steadily nearer to the area where the guns were in action. The shots became more intermittent, but the cries grew in volume and he had the distinct impression that the gunmen were engaged in some kind of sport rather than in a gun battle.

Ten minutes' riding brought him to a narrow winding valley between two scrub-covered ridges, and there he dismounted, hauling his Winchester from the scabbard. He led the horse by the head until the valley opened out and there he left it in the last of the natural cover, its reins snagged over a bush.

Three minutes of crouched running

and occasional pauses brought him to a small cluster of rocks from which he could see a mound fringed around the top by high clumps of grass. Five men were in a loose circle about the top of the mound with six-guns in their hands.

While he toyed with his shoulder weapon, a revolver was discharged. The echoes were still busy when a man cried out in anguish.

'That's enough! If I knew anything more I'd tell you, but I don't! So why don't you leave me in peace, if you intend me to die here? After all that shootin' you're due for company, an' you know it!'

There was a chorus of jeering laughter. A tall lean man in a dark riding outfit, who had his back to Chris' position, was one of two gunmen to fire again. Still puzzled about the incident, Chris decided that the time had come to take a hand. The voice he had heard was a strange one to him, but that did not deter him.

He put the Winchester to his

shoulder, rested the barrel on a rock surface and took careful aim. The first bullet flew a foot over the head of the man in black. The sudden crack of the weapon transformed the scene ahead. Two men whose heads and shoulders had been in view to right and left of the mound top disappeared with some show of alacrity. The black garbed man stiffened momentarily and then suddenly dived head first over the high grass. His boots were the last of him to go to earth, but Chris did not notice them as he was panning his weapon around and firing again.

While the rifle bullets were making the position unhealthy, the outlaws — quite used to sudden changes of fortune — were hurriedly withdrawing. A sharp order was issued. A rifle and two six-guns returned the unexpected fire, but it was clear by the way in which they were aimed that no one had any clear idea of where the shots had come from.

Jake Dollar was as surprised as his

tormentors. He had not expected any outside interference and he had no means of knowing whether a posse had stumbled upon them, or whether the intruder was just someone who had blundered on the uneven contest and decided to take a hand.

While Ringo and Bummer were returning the gun fire, the prisoner squirmed tiredly against his bonds and wondered what the future had in store for him. Pinned out as he was, he had just endured one of the most terrifying experiences of his life.

Most of the bullets aimed at loosening his tongue had passed under his body, making grooves in the loose soil. Two or three had singed his shirt which was thoroughly wet with his perspiration. His normally arrogant expression was missing. The pallor created by fear showed under his sunburned skin.

He blinked salt sweat out of his eyes and watched the movements of his tormentors, wondering what they were going to do with him, if anything.

While the exchanges were still going on, Long Tom, who was good at making split-second decisions, hesitated for a moment. The leader himself hurled the telltale red trunk away into bushes on lower ground and directed his brother to bring along the stocky corpse.

'I don't see why I should have to tote the body along with me!' Nate protested.

'Do as you're told!' Tom snapped, and that put an end to the arguing. 'Put up another few shots and then follow the rest of us!' he ordered brusquely.

Without waiting any longer he led the way down the back slope of the mound to where their horses awaited them, closely followed by Colorado and his brother, who was dragging the body. Smith saw to his cinch straps and then turned to assist Nate, who was cursing breathlessly under his burden.

It was not easy to get the corpse across the back of a saddle, but between them they managed it. Almost at once, Ringo and Bummer came slithering down the slope after them. There was nearly a minute of apparent chaos among the horses before they were all mounted up.

While they were busy with their withdrawal routine, Dollar strained to get his neck and shoulders high enough to see what they were doing. Clearly, they had no immediate plans for him. He was grateful that no one had thought to put a final bullet in him. Now, he had to await the approach of the intruder, or intruders, if there happened to be more than one.

His throat was parched. If he had still had the red cloth stuffed in his mouth during the recent happenings he might have choked to death. He lowered his head, closed his eyes against the burning sun and tried to calm himself.

The sounds of horses hooves and the noises of mounted men pushing through undergrowth soon faded, but the other sounds which he expected were slow to materialise. After a time lapse of about three minutes, he began to perspire all over again.

He began to call out. 'Help! You down there with the rifle! It's all right to come up here now!'

Chris came up slowly. He was taking his time and moving quite warily. It was one thing to disturb a bunch of wild gunmen and another thing to be taken by surprise himself in such an isolated spot. Just when Dollar expected him to show himself, he made a half circuit of the exposed position and came up on the other side.

Dollar had been under observation for upwards of ten seconds when he first set eyes upon his deliverer. His slanted green orbs studied the new-comer almost avidly, taking in every visible detail and wondering if this young sandy-haired interloper had any personal interest in the recent exchanges.

'Mister, I owe you my life. I don't know how you happened along jest when you did, but that bunch of gunmen were set on shootin' the living daylights out of me!'

He paused, wondering what sort of reaction to expect. Chris remained looking down at him from five or six feet away, equally curious about the pegged-out prisoner.

'If you ask me, amigo, they were takin' their time about it. Maybe they didn't intend to kill you at all. I could be forgiven for surmisin' that they were playin' games with you.'

The voice was calm, betokening a determined self-reliant character. Dollar's first summing-up was that this was no outlaw. A man on the right side of the law, but no evidence of a lawman's badge.

'You'll allow the games were not the kind ordinary folks play on their friends. I'd be obliged if you'd put yourself about a bit more an' cut me loose. It ain't beyond the bounds of possibility that my enemies might return.'

Dollar regarded Chris, breathless and open-mouthed. Chris knew that the advice was good. If the outlaws, as he supposed the others to be, did decide to return, he would have to share their wrath with the man with the peculiar features, features which he had already recognised.

'My knife is somewhere down that slope over there,' Dollar prompted hopefully.

Reluctantly, Chris went across to find it. As he came back up the slope with the knife in his hand, he remarked: 'I've seen your face before. Quite recently.'

Dollar gasped. He refrained from commenting and gradually relaxed as his leg bonds and then those which secured his wrists were severed. Rather wearily, he drew himself together, rubbing the sore places and eyeing the knife which had done the deed.

He approached Chris, wanting to shake his hand but the younger man backed off and intimated that he was not keen on such things.

He said: 'Jack Doolin, alias James

Delange, alias Jake Dollar. Which are you today?'

'Oh, Jake, I guess. Call me Jake. And don't think the worst of me. Is it all right for me to go an' look for my hardware now? We may not have much time.'

'Okay, but remember I know all the details on that reward notice in Silver City, so don't try any fast tricks on me.'

Dollar scurried off in the direction where he had seen his guns tossed and presently he came back again and threw himself down in the grass. He was pleased because his horse was still available to him and his guns were undamaged, but he was wary of this young man who knew so much about his past. Chris also hunkered down, but he kept in such a position that Dollar was a little forward of him, so that a surprise could readily be countered. Dollar took the spyglass which was offered him.

'Who were the outlaws who attacked you, Dollar?'

Dollar blinked, but continued his examination of the terrain in the direction of the gang's departure. 'They were the Breeze gang. Long Tom Breeze, his brother, Nate, and three others. Maybe you'd answer a question for me now. You don't appear to be a peace officer of any sort. Why do you take such an interest in notices about me?'

'I'm Chris Morgan, if you need to know. Recently out of the United States cavalry.'

Chris paused, having reminded himself of something he had almost forgotten in the rush of events since he came into the county. He had just recollected that one or two units working out of Fort Comanche, to the north, were intending to come south into Conchas County, New Mexico, on manoeuvres. He wondered if he was likely to run across any of them and whether they would be in a position to help him in his self-appointed tasks. Presently, he decided that he was drumming up forlorn hopes. He put the cavalry out of his mind and addressed himself further to his questioner.

'Two men left the hotel in Silver City about the same time. I was interested in the other one. You only interest me because your trail might have crossed that of my friend, Crossdraw Willie Lester. If you know anything about Willie, you could save yourself a whole lot of grief by sayin' so right now.'

Dollar had never thought faster. His quick wittedness showed him a way out of his present difficulties. He chuckled.

'Well, what do you know? I came to assist Crossdraw Willie, an' you came to town to do the same. I don't rightly know where he is now, but I was lookin' for him to do him a favour.'

Chris was expected to ask excitedly what the favour was, but his unlined face reflected nothing but suspicion as he glared at the slant-eyed man and waited for him to go on.

'I was figurin' on showin' Willie the way into the robbers' hideout back there in the foothills. Now, admit that surprises you!'

Chris sniffed. 'If it's true, it surprises me. How come Willie left town in such mysterious circumstances around the same time that you did?'

Dollar raised his palms in an open-handed gesture calculated to disarm his suspicious listener. 'How do I know the answer to that, amigo? Maybe somebody gave him a tip-off. Understand that for my part, I had to play it cool. Not show myself too much, on account of my unsavoury past. When it occurred to me that the Professor had left town without sayin' a word to anybody, I came out this way lookin' for him.'

'You didn't find him, but you ran into the Breeze outfit. Why was it they were so rough on you, Dollar?'

'Because they thought I knew the location of some old loot,' the other answered, toying with his soiled derby. Most of his life was based on lies, but he did not hesitate to use the truth when he thought it would benefit him. 'Do you believe that?'

Chris thought about the question for a few seconds. He nodded his head. Presently, he indicated that the two of them were going back in an easterly direction for a short distance to recover a horse. Dollar started off five yards ahead, aware that he was still on trial, even though he had his weapons.

He called back over his shoulder. 'If you're thinkin' of shootin' me in the back or anything, amigo, I wouldn't do that. After all, if we don't locate Crossdraw Willie I could always show you the way into the robber's roost.'

Chris was very thoughtful about Dollar's flippant remarks. He wondered why Dollar should think of being shot in the back. Was there anything on his conscience which would prompt anyone to shoot him in the back?

They found the stockingfoot where it had been left and returned with it to the spot where the outlaws had left Dollar's heavily-boned dun. At that point, each man checked over his saddle and harness and prepared to mount up.

'You must have heard me when I made you an offer back there, Chris,' Dollar remarked pointedly.

Chris swung into leather. 'I know what Willie was plannin' to do, mister. Right now, though, I'm more interested in his reappearance than anything else.'

Dollar also swung up into his saddle. His thoughts were in a chaotic turmoil. For once in his life, he had no clear plan of action.

7

The next two hours saw the two ill-assorted riders moving slowly and cautiously south-west of the position where Dollar had been left by the outlaws. The afternoon was well advanced. Each man seemed more aware of his riding partner than of the need to ride in any specific direction.

Chris Morgan was in a quandary. He thought that Jake Dollar knew far more about Willie Lester's movements than he had so far revealed. Morover, he had a very clear idea of what a tricky customer he was dealing with. Had he not thought that Dollar had more useful information for him, he would have acted very differently.

Dollar, for his part, did not know what sort of a ploy would best suit his immediate ends. Clearly, Morgan mistrusted him, but so long as Morgan thought there was anything to be gained from keeping company with him, he was useful as an ally, however reluctant.

When they had been riding for an hour, Chris tried a few more questions.

'Why are you takin' me in this direction, Jake?'

The man in the derby hat shrugged. He forced a crooked grin and hesitated before committing himself. 'The fact is, Chris, I don't rightly know. I had such a going over by the Breeze boys my thoughts are a bit scrambled right now. I suppose without knowin' it I wanted to get away from that place where the shootin' took place.

'I don't reckon we're anywhere near the gang at this moment. An' then there's that other consideration. Like I said, I could undertake to show you the way into the robbers' roost. I figure I owe you something, an' that would be a way of repayin' you. Have you thought any more about that proposition?'

Chris cleared his dry throat. 'Have you thought any more about what I said

the last time? I mean about findin'
Crossdraw Willie first?'

Dollar clearly hesitated, but at that
time he was not prepared to make any
further revelations, and so the riding
went on. Around two hours after they
had first mounted up, they were riding
across a patch of high ground when
Dollar happened to glance towards the
north. To his surprise he caught sight
of several figures on horseback riding
in a single file across another ridge.

He glanced in Chris' direction,
confirmed that his partner had not seen
the riders, and then decided that the
time had come to divulge further
information. The riders in question
were soldiers: some kind of a cavalry
detail, probably out on manoeuvres of
some sort. Morgan might or might not
know about their presence in the
district.

Dollar had no wish to confront the
cavalry. To the east Silver City was
unhealthy for him. Maybe he ought to
tell about Willie Lester's fate and hope

that Morgan would stay sympathetic towards him.

As they rode down off the high ground and negotiated a well grassed hollow broken up by stunted trees, he swung his leg out of leather and slid to the ground, reaching for his water canteen. Chris, who had been a yard or two behind him, slowed down and did the same, showing no enthusiasm.

Dollar seated himself on a small rock and indicated a fallen log opposite to him. Chris hesitated before sitting down rather gingerly on the moss-covered tree bole.

'I don't know what changed your mind, but I have the feelin' you've decided to tell me something. Goodness knows you've had time enough to cook up a good story. Make it good, huh?'

Dollar coughed on a mouthful of water.

'I take it you were pretty close to Willie Lester. Would it bother you a lot if you knew you wouldn't see him any more?'

Chris gripped his canteen until his knuckles showed white through the skin. Subconsciously, he had known that Willie might have been eliminated, but he had always turned his thoughts away from such a consideration.

'You're hintin' that he might be dead,' he accused. 'If that's what you have in mind, convince me. Don't tell me half a story. An' tell it fast!'

The canteen shook in his fist. Dollar seemed fascinated by it until Chris recovered himself a little and carefully laid it down beside him.

Dollar swallowed hard. 'I know he's dead because I saw his body. The Breeze gang had it with them. One of them fixed him with a knife. I guess it was a throwing knife.'

Chris' jaw line hardened even more. It was clear by the look on his face that he did not want to believe in his friend's death. In addition, he was in a dangerous mood.

'How come you lied so glibly in concealin' the news of Willie's death from me after I cut you loose?'

Dollar waved his hands in a gesture intended to be conciliatory.

'Bear in mind I'd had rather a bad time. I didn't figure you were ready to take the shock at that time. When you opened up on the gang, Long Tom decided to take the corpse along with him. An' that's a fact!'

'Why would he take it along with him if he thought his life was in danger? Answer me that!'

Dollar sighed. 'You claim to know what Willie's main ambition was, to penetrate the stronghold back there. Maybe you don't know there was a price on his head.'

This latter suggestion prompted the younger man to rise swiftly to his feet and advance a step. Dollar watched him warily and did not relax again until Chris corked his canteen and gave out with a dry laugh completely devoid of humour.

'Now I know you're puttin' me on, Dollar. We're talkin' about a federal officer not a common outlaw. Who would be in a position to put a price on his head?'

Dollar took the question seriously. 'Someone with a lot of power an' influence outside the law who stood to lose by the marshal's future plans. I speak of the boss of the hideout, one Colonel Herman Clervaux, a southern gentleman who turned sour on society when the Confederacy lost the war.'

Chris had heard the name before, but no one had ever confirmed that the former Confederate officer was indeed the brains behind the outlaw's hideout. His green eyes were roving over his restless partner, inch by inch, seeing him and not seeing him as his groping mind assessed the implications of Dollar's latest revelation.

'An' now you're saying this Long Tom Breeze is takin' a corpse into the hideout to collect the reward for the killin'?'

Dollar nodded. Chris moved away from him, his brain busy with new considerations, new conclusions. Although he appeared to be fully absorbed, there was something in his manner which prevented Dollar from seizing an opportunity to get the drop on him. Five minutes elapsed, during which the wily Dollar could only guess at his thought processes.

When Chris was ready to talk again, he was still firmly in control of the situation.

'All right, assumin' there's some truth in what you've been tellin' me, I intend to look further into the matter myself. I believe you have a very shrewd idea where that other outfit headed by Long Tom Breeze could be located at this time, or in an hour or two.

'You're goin' to put me in touch with them an' I'm not standin' for any arguments! Is that understood?'

Dollar nodded with sufficient enthusiasm to make Chris believe that he could and would discover the outlaws' whereabouts, provided that he stayed under pressure.

★   ★   ★

About the same time, the Breeze outfit of renegade riders was some two miles further westward and equally in need of rest and refreshment. Nate Breeze's wilting skewbald was blowing hard due to its efforts with a double load. Once again, the younger Breeze was the first to openly complain.

'Doggone it, big brother, we've been pushin' it hard for nigh on two hours! In that time we've seen no signs of the jasper who blasted off at us back there! It sure is time we hit the earth an' took a rest. As for this dead lawman, some other sort of arrangements will have to be made! I'm finished with him an' that's final!'

Long Tom, who had a nice sense of his own dignity and rather subtle ways of maintaining his superiority, rode on for another fifty yards before he showed that he had heard his brother's complaint. He was aware that Colorado, Bummer and Ringo were watching him when he topped the rim of a small flat plateau and noted a still pool near the middle of it.

'All right, boys, you can dismount here. But don't throw caution to the winds! Remember we've been caught unawares once today! It had better not happen again. Next time, we might not be so lucky!'

Nate was the first to hit the ground. He hauled the dead body unceremoniously out of his saddle and showed little heed when the skewbald kicked and reared and backed away from it. One after another the others swung clear of leather and tiredly dropped to the ground.

Nate massaged his red face with a chequered bandanna and scowled at his partners, who kept their expressions away from Long Tom. One by one, the horses went in search of water, while the riders mopped themselves down and eased their damp shirts away from their backs. Long Tom's bright yellow bandanna changed its colour as he worked on his neck and face with it.

'So what do you make of things, boys?' Tom asked, conversationally.

Nate snorted and began to think of words in which to express his disgust about the way in which they had been panicked earlier.

'I'm askin' Ringo', Tom put in, before Nate could speak.

Ringo nodded, flashed a brief smile and went through the motions of flapping his black bolero and rocking his steeple hat. 'I think we have to assume that Dollar had a friend somewhere in the district. There might have been more than one gun hostile to us, but I don't think so. If there had been a large number, they might have pursued us. If there was only one, Jake wouldn't have wanted jest the two of them to come after us. He would not go against five with only one to back him.'

Breeze acknowledged the Mexican's

opinion and glanced at the others. Colorado intimated that he thought along the same lines, and Bummer merely nodded. Nate maintained a stubborn silence.

Colorado, whose heavy moustache was itching due to perspiration, added: 'I don't think it would be wise to try an' take the body all the way into the stronghold. It's heavy. Time's passin' an' it wants plantin'. There must be some way in which we can put forward a claim without takin' the corpse with us.'

'How about takin' along those two fancy shootin' irons?' Gorten suggested tentatively. 'After all, they do have Lester's initials stamped into the butt plates.'

'Good thinkin', Bummer,' the red-headed leader enthused. 'We'll bury him right here before we move on. I'd like for you an' Ringo to take first turn with the spades. Find a spot where the soil is easy.'

There was a slight delay of a minute

or more while the disgruntled four adjusted to the latest orders. The small Mexican was the first to make a move. He was prodding the earth with a spade blade before anyone else reacted. Bummer joined him and was soon out of breath. In the meantime, Long Tom gave his sweating stallion a light but thorough grooming. Colorado covered his face with his stetson and dozed. Brother Nate lay stretched out flat on his back with his eyes closed and a brown paper cigarette smoking between his lips.

When the grooming of the stallion was completed, Long Tom took off his stetson and put a comb through his flattened ginger hair. His beard and sideburns were given the same treatment before he turned his thoughts to progress. On the face of things, Ringo and Bummer had chosen a good spot to dig, but less than eighteen inches below the surface they were slowed by fragments of rock.

'You two diggers hand over your

tools to Nate an' Colorado, an' before you settle down take a look around through a spyglass. As I said before, we can't afford to be reckless — especially when we've been caught out once in the day.'

The second team of diggers showed no enthusiasm. Once again, the Mexican complied first, leaving the shaded area and going towards higher ground. Bummer made as if to follow him, but Ringo indicated a second mound about fifty yards away from the one he was heading for. Shrugging wearily, the paunchy outlaw changed direction. His grey sideburns were dripping with perspiration and he had forgotten to take a spyglass with him.

Much experience of guerrilla tactics made Ringo cautious on occasions like this. No sooner was his battered steeple hat clear of the surrounding grass than he knew they were in for trouble. There was considerable movement to eastward and not very far distant. Through the glass a short column of cavalry troopers came into focus. He could see upwards of six riders heading almost directly towards their position.

He pursed his lips and snapped his fingers to attract the attention of his fellow lookout, who was still toiling up the other mound. Bummer heard the signal and pretended to ignore it. In the meantime, Ringo turned his glass to right and left and discovered another column, riding parallel with the first one.

His expression hardened. He snapped his fingers three times in quick succession. Bummer then realised that he had forgotten to bring a glass along, but to his shocked surprise he was able to see the column opposite to him without artificial aid.

He was badly out of breath when he rejoined the others on the plateau and made straight for his pinto which reacted to his presence without enthusiasm.

'Two columns of pony soldiers, Boss,' Ringo reported. 'Heading straight for us about two hundred yards apart. There's a lieutenant at the head of one group an' a corporal leadin' the other. We've got to move fast.'

Colorado and Nate stopped digging at once and hurried over to listen.

'They could be jest practisin' but they look like men with a definite plan in view,' Ringo added. 'They might number up to a score.'

'Think they know about us?' Nate murmured nervously.

'They may not know where we are, but we have to assume they know about our attack on the stage. The lawmen work very closely with the army these days,' Tom opined gravely.

'Leave the diggin'. We leave the corpse behind. Get ready to mount up an' make no noise. Is that understood?'

No one argued. Tom, himself, collected the crossdraw gun belt and the hardware that went with it. He packed them away in his saddle pockets and pointed towards the south-west.

8

Purely by chance, Dollar led Chris Morgan on to the plateau by the south-east corner not five minutes after the outlaws had withdrawn. Within seconds the newcomers had noticed the newly turned mound of earth and Chris moved ahead, prompted by anxiety.

He leapt out of leather five yards from the intended grave and was on his knees beside the crumpled figure almost at once. He recognised Willard Lester immediately in spite of the changes wrought in his appearance.

Dollar, blissfully unaware of the nearness of the soldiers, saw this as an opportunity to be rid of his temporary ally. Chris was still quietly bemoaning his friend's demise and had not removed his stetson when a revolver barrel connected with the side of his head and dropped him unconscious across the body of the man whom he had sought so avidly.

The man with the slanted eyes was breathless with the sudden changes of fortune. He saw the freshly dug grave as a receptacle for the body of his earlier victim and also that of young Morgan who, to him, was a potential source of danger.

Thinking that he had time in hand, he dragged the federal marshal's body to the edge of the pit, not troubling himself about the noise he made. Uppermost in his mind was how he should dispose of Morgan. He was standing over the unconscious ex-cavalryman with his lethal blade to hand when he heard the bolt of a shoulder weapon click quite close.

He looked up and saw a rifle pointed at him from less than forty yards away. Lieutenant Max Stride, in charge of the cavalry detail, had caught a glimpse of Bummer Gorten's shapeless stetson before the latter withdrew. Six troopers had dismounted and crawled towards the plateau unobserved.

Two other troopers, several yards on either side of the first one to show himself, rose slowly to their feet with their weapons pointing. Dollar dropped his knife and stood to one side, making it apparent that his hands were empty and that he had no intention of making any sort of false move.

★　★　★

Chris Morgan recovered his senses rather slowly. His head was singing due to the blow on the head and he had no clear idea of the incidents prior to his unconsciousness. His head was supported on a man's knee while a water canteen was applied to his lips.

He spluttered on the water and stiffened, staring up into the face above his own. It was a familiar one: one which he had thought to be many miles away. That of his brother, Corporal Bart Morgan, newly promoted.

'Well, howdy, brother,' Bart murmured, 'it sure looks as if you needed help when we found you.'

Chris nodded carefully and grinned. He studied the familiar features and noted the concern in the pale blue eyes which gave the lie to the quizzical grin. Bart Morgan scarcely looked his twenty-three years. Out of uniform he could pass almost for a youth in his teens.

Max Stride, the officer in charge, strolled over to take a look at Chris while the latter was still recovering. The army party was from Fort Comanche. All of them were known to Chris due to his army time spent at the fort.

Stride had a pair of riding gauntlets in one hand and a small crumpled note in the other. He was a strict young officer of thirty years. In appearance he had struck fear into many a new recruit. He had black tufts of hair on his cheekbones, a lantern jaw and bleak grey eyes. His mouth was small. The thin lips were scarcely visible.

'Well, Chris, I sure am sorry to find you in such circumstances. Tell me, did you and this fellow in the derby hat dig that grave?'

Chris pushed aside the water canteen and peered around him, thirsting for information. 'No, lieutenant, we didn't dig it. A bunch of outlaws must have done it. Almost certainly a group headed by a man named Long Tom Breeze. They must have had Federal Marshal Lester's body with them, too. I've been lookin' for him all over the county, an' now I find him dead.'

Stride showed no surprise when the identity of the dead man was mentioned. He toyed with the paper in his hand, bent and offered it to Chris with a brief smile.

'You nearly joined Lester in death, amigo. Your partner was about to eliminate you before fillin' that grave with both your bodies. Here, take a look at this note. I found it in the lining of the deceased man's hat. Other searchers must have overlooked it.'

126

Chris freed himself from his brother's support and took the note rather gingerly. While he studied the brief letter written on it, his brother and Stride remarked to one another about his admiration for the old lawman and his ambition to be of service to him.

The note was in Nerena Lester's handwriting. Chris recognised it because she had once written to him. The date put the time of writing at five weeks earlier than the present. For a time, the purport of the letter erased all recent happenings from his mind.

Dear Uncle Will,

You, of all people, will find this hard to understand. It has come to my notice that Colonel Herman Clervaux is in bad health and needs immediate medical aid. I have thought the matter over at some length and decided to offer my services. Don't think too badly of me, and try to remember that a good doctor is supposed to minister to anyone who needs him.

Don't go taking on too much. Don't fret over me. Give my warm regards to Chris Morgan when you see him.

Your wilful but affectionate niece Nerena. X

Chris gave out with a sigh which sounded almost like a groan. He handed the note to his brother and slowly scrambled to his feet. With Lieutenant Stride pacing easily beside him, he walked away from the grave which he had almost occupied. He rubbed his head, trying to bring himself up to date.

Stride was patient with him. Chris had briefly acknowledged several old friends who were relaxing on the grassed area before the officer began the exchange of information.

'Does the Colonel mentioned in that letter mean anything to you, Chris?'

'I've heard it said by Dollar, the man who was with me, that Clervaux is the top man in the robbers' hideout west of here. The only interpretation I can put on Nerena's letter is that she has gone herself into the hideout to give Clervaux medical attention. There's no wonder Willie Lester was in such a hurry to have the roost turned over, once and for all.'

'I agree with you. In case you didn't know, Marshal Lester made certain of his needs known to the fort Commandant, and when our Colonel checked with a higher authority he was ordered to give full support to any scheme mooted by Lester. A senator with a famous name had a hand in the plans.'

'I didn't know that,' Chris confessed, 'but I can tell you what one of my main reasons for leavin' the cavalry when I did was to side Lester when he flushed out the outlaws. Now that he's dead, I fully intend to take on his commitments.'

Stride coughed and came to a halt between two stunted trees.

'If the government and the camp

commandant knew Lester was dead, army support for the campaign might be withdrawn. Right now, no one other than us an' a few outlaws know Lester's out of the fight. You are here, an' we are here an' you can count on us for any amount of worthwhile support.'

Chris stopped massaging the bump on his head and shook hands with his new ally. 'Right now, the Breeze gang will most likely be on their way into the strong-hold. I aim to use Dollar to show me the way, otherwise it might take months.'

Stride nodded. 'I suppose you've no alternative but to use him. Maybe I ought to tell my men to ease off him a bit.'

In answer to Chris' puzzled look of enquiry, the lieutenant took him along to a nearby hollow where Dollar was seen to be on tiptoe and hatless, trying with great fortitude to keep the noose around his neck from stopping his breath altogether. Above his head the rope snaked over a tree branch and went away in a taut line to where a trooper sat his horse with the end secured to his saddle horn.

The army was expressing its disapproval of his treatment of one of their kind.

Dollar spotted Chris' approach at once. He turned his head a little, hoping to shout something but he was near to choking in his efforts and one of his boot toes slipped on an uneven rock making things worse.

'We need him alive, and I don't think he'll stay scared for long,' Chris murmured.

Stride signalled to the trooper who allowed the rope to slacken a little. Dollar used the brief respite to regain his breath. He was in a sorry condition and he did not know if the treatment would be renewed.

'Only one thing keeps you alive, Dollar,' Chris called out to the sufferer, 'knowin' the way into the stronghold. The army would be happy to see you dead, accidentally killed on manoeuvres, so think yourself lucky an' act accordingly.'

Without haste, Dollar was released under escort. Two troopers put the deceased into his grave and the uniformed party went through their preparations for moving out. Following a little ceremony around the burial mound, the cavalry mounted up. Chris exchanged a few last words with his brother, Bart, as though he did not expect to meet him for quite a time.

Chris mounted up and exchanged salutes as in the old days. The troopers clattered off the plateau shouting personal farewells. Dollar, with his red cloth lightly tied round his aching neck, noted that they went towards the south.

The two men remaining exchanged hard glances. Finally, Chris tossed down the killer's hand guns, having extracted the bullets from them. The throwing knife was also returned, minus its point.

'You're livin' on borrowed time, pardner,' Chris remarked dryly. 'Take us into the hideout, an' take care how you behave.'

Dollar mounted his dun with what dignity he could muster. He was surprised that Chris had not guessed that *he* had killed Lester, and not Long Tom Breeze.

★   ★   ★

A narrow creek marked the beginnings of the true approaches to the robbers' roost. On the westward side of it for several miles stretched a desolate area of low volcanic rock foothills rendered treacherous in places by unsuspected patches of boggy turf.

The first inroads into Colonel Clervaux's territory had to be made along the course of a dried-out stream which ran across the formidable morass in a westerly direction. Not many intruders had ever located the *arroyo* in Clervaux's time and those who had, had paid the penalty at the other end, due to the renegades' splendid vigilance on a fine natural mesa which overlooked it.

One of the rules of the hideout was that any incoming mob or gang, fresh from marauding expeditions in the surrounding territories, had to take over the mesa top as lookouts and relieve the men already up there. On arrival in the commanding position, any outside information thought to be worth repeating connected with recent exploits, or having a possible bearing upon future exploits, had to be sent along to the hideout headquarters, to be relayed by the retiring guards.

Late the following day, Long Tom Breeze and his boys successfully negotiated the approach *arroyo*. Long Tom himself broke away from the rest of his group, riding deliberately close to certain geographical features so that those who watched on the high eminence would know that he had been there before, and that he knew the routine.

In the last hour of daylight, the five riders worked their way up on to the top of the mesa and were at once surrounded by seven men who made up the gang of one Frisco 'T' James, a man with a brown bush of beard, a 't' shaped scar on one cheek and a bald head. Frisco had the reputation of doing his best work with dynamite, but he had not figured much in the newspapers of late due to a shortage of that deadly commodity.

Three items of information were mentioned over the boosted supper fires that night. One was concerning the death of Federal Marshal Lester. The second had to do with the strike against the stagecoach headed for South Pass. The third was a routine message about army cavalry units on practice manoeuvres in the territory to the east.

9

Saddle rations and the strain of not being able to trust his companion began to have an effect upon Chris Morgan, but he kept his doubts and his ill-humours to himself as Dollar preceded him along the *arroyo* on another afternoon, and rejoiced that Jake had brought him along the first of the roundabout route to get in.

For upwards of an hour, Chris had given the impression that he was wilting in the saddle, not far from sleep. During that time, he had watched his wily guide very closely. Dollar's actions and the interest he showed in the terrain right ahead of them convinced young Morgan that his partner was more interested in making progress rather than attempting some clever trick to regain his freedom.

Around five o'clock, Dollar insisted

on a halt and Chris at once agreed. Neither of them looked very present-able. Dollar's brown hat had been dented several times during recent incidents. His white shirt was crumpled and grey. The black string tie which had once adorned his neck was now discarded. He wore his shirt collar open and his red square of cloth was folded and worn loosely like a bandanna, concealing the bruised flesh, hurt when the noose had stretched him.

Dollar had taken a lot of knocks from a lot of people, but he was not down-hearted and he promised himself that if he got half a chance he would lie and scheme to bring about the downfall of all those who had crossed him. He drank from his water canteen and afterwards smacked his lips as though it had been cool beer. The thin line of his brown moustache, normally trimmed quite regularly, was thickening and becoming ragged in shape. Stubble the colour of his sunburnt skin subtly altered the line of his jaw.

Action seemed to have matured Chris. His lighter, sandy hair grew faster than that of Dollar. Since he had shaved last the beginnings of a beard had outlined his lower features like an extension of his sideburns. The crows-feet wrinkles at the outer ends of his eyes appeared to have deepened.

'Unless my eyes are deceivin' me, Jake, there could be a man on top of that mesa right ahead,' Chris remarked brusquely. 'I hope that when we go on you'll make all the right moves because bein' in your company has not endeared you to me. You've pulled too many fast ones in your life for me to hesitate before shootin' you in the back!'

Dollar gargled with a mouthful of water. 'I know it sounds silly me usin' the word trust, but you'll have to leave things to me when we get closer. I haven't been through the defences for a while. All I know is the routine which was in force the last time I came.

'Believe me, there's many a jasper

ahead of us I'd far rather see dead than you, so take heart. Most hombres who come this far along Clervaux's private track end up dead before the day is out. With me, you stand a chance of survivin' an' that has to mean something!'

Before they started forward again, Chris found himself brooding over that letter discovered by Lieutenant Stride. 'Did you ever hear tell of a woman in the hideout, Jake? Does the Colonel have his own staff in there?'

The slant-eyed man whistled in surprise. He wondered what had prompted such a question and seemed impressed by Chris's desire for a serious answer.

'I ain't never seen any woman in there, amigo. No woman at all! Why, the Colonel wouldn't hear of such a thing. I figure he's right when he says women only stir up trouble in circumstances like he faces in the hideout.' He regarded Chris with his head on one side. Some of his old arrogance returned in his manner. 'If you think Clervaux would permit women you have no idea at all about discipline — an' you an ex-cavalryman not long released!'

Chris ignored the taunt. 'Maybe it's because the old Colonel is too old to be interested in women for himself. But what about his second in command? He must delegate some authority to someone. How does the *segundo* feel about women?'

'You mean Frenchy Lafitte, of course. Well, Frenchy is a good lookin' fellow but he doesn't have the authority to thwart the old man an' as Frenchy is more or less a fixture on the inside, he has to do without the feminine charms. Poor Frenchy, I never did figure out that side of his life. I don't think I'd want to change mine for his.'

Dollar had no idea what was behind Chris's curious questioning. He stopped giving out information after a while, concluding that Morgan was simply pumping him for information that might be of use in the future, always providing that he survived long enough to get into the stronghold proper.

Dollar thought of all the possible hazards which lay ahead of Morgan, some laid on by the defenders of the place and others thought up on the spur of the moment by himself. Morgan, he concluded, was an unusual young fellow for his years, but he was also an incurable and rather stupid optimist. His days were undoubtedly numbered.

* * *

Half an hour later, perspiration began to glisten at the back of Dollar's neck. Chris perceived this and also a slight slowing down in forward progress. He knew enough about his guide to know that he did not get a sticky neck on account of anyone else. Dollar was worried for himself.

His attention was more often directed

to the top of the mesa which commanded a view of the approach route rather than anywhere else. It was an obvious spot on which to have a regular lookout and guard.

'One thing I'm sure of, Jake, you don't have the look of a man ridin' in to meet long lost friends. It's clear to me that a man or some men on that mesa top have us under observation. So what do we do now, fire a few friendly shots?'

'No, we don't. The men on the mesa are likely to be the Breeze gang. Pretty soon now, I'm goin' to diverge towards the south-west. Whatever happens, don't follow me. You'd be too much of a target in daylight. If you have to take avoidin' action, go the other way an' keep your head down.'

'I gather there isn't much future in goin' to the north-west of the mesa,' Chris commented calmly.

'That's so. If you do try the south-westerly route, wait until dark. That way you might stand a chance. The most direct route into the hideout is due north of the mesa. Anyone goin' in by that route has to negotiate a narrow stream. An' there'll be lookouts, closer in. I can't tell you any way to beat the defence system. It's too complicated for one man, an' in any case what I know of it is probably out of date.'

Before Chris could think up any suitable reply, a heavy calibre weapon fired in their direction from the mesa top. A shot from a buffalo gun whined over their heads at long range.

Dollar muttered excitedly. 'That was the warnin' shot! I told you the boys up there wouldn't be friendly! I'm going to cut off to the left real soon. When I go you cut off to the right. Find cover an' watch out for marshy ground! You got that?'

Dollar had increased his dun's pace. Chris did the same, experiencing some of the old excitement of a cavalry trooper riding into action.

Three rifles opened up at extreme range and that was the signal for Jake

Dollar to make his own move. He crouched in the saddle, yelling mock Indian war whoops and abruptly turned his mount off the regular trail, lurching over the rim of the *arroyo* and dropping out of sight almost at once.

A bullet grooved dirt just ahead of the startled roan, causing it to roar and flail the air with its white stockinged leg. Chris kept his saddle with difficulty, hauling the frightened beast around on its hind legs and heading it for the nearest cluster of rocks beyond the banking.

He made it as two well-aimed shells came probing for the jinxing target. One ricocheted off rock and the other passed between the horse's weaving legs. Filling his lungs, he yelled at the roan and succeeded in bringing it to a spectacular stop just short of two overlapping rocks which would have required a good leap to clear them off soft earth.

Chris slipped to his knees and allowed his lungs to get back to normal.

The hostile firing stopped almost as suddenly as it had started. As the gun shot echoes faded, the diminishing sounds of Dollar's horse emphasised the loneliness and extreme vulnerability of the young rider's position. To pass a few minutes and at the same time calm himself, he went through his saddle pockets and took stock of the food which remained to him. Among other items was a first-class spyglass which one of the troopers must have put there unknown to him.

He was reminded that Lieutenant Stride and others were in sympathy with what he was trying to do. It was not beyond the bounds of probability that the soldiers would keep in touch, but what could Stride's men, a mere sub-troop intended for scouting or general reconnaissance, do against a fortress manned by desperate men assisted greatly by the local geography?

Had there been a full troop of sixty men, backed up by gatlings and extra transport animals such as mules, the army might stand a chance with the element of surprise behind them.

Chris sighed. The silence continued. It began to seem as if Dollar's approach would not be further contested. He began to wonder if he would see the tricky killer ever again. Maybe those in the stronghold proper had more confidence in the lone assassin than the outlaws he had encountered more recently.

Conjecture was not worth while at this stage. Using the spyglass Chris learned as much as he could about the unfamiliar terrain around him. Not many yards north of the *arroyo* the soil appeared to be vastly more moist than elsewhere. A few minutes of crawling and crouching between rocks revealed another phenomenon. To the north-east of the mesa, the rock and bog region gave way to scorched earth. At one time, the grass might have grown to a useful height, perhaps high enough to conceal crawling men, but recently all the grass and all growing things had been burned off it. Any human or sizeable animal seeking to cross the scorched earth would show up easily to the watchers on the mesa with the blackened stubble forming a dark backcloth.

Chris shook his head about that region and returned to the rocks overlooking the *arroyo* side. There, the ground undulated and the grass was intact. Moreover, it was of a natural colour as if the boggy quality of the subsoil did not extend that far.

Scattered about the area was a good deal of grey and black rock. Prominent among the bigger rocks was a cylindrical stone formation of an unusual shape. In its infancy, many hundreds of years ago, it had been almost completely conical. Since then, time and weather had scooped away much of its substance some seventy feet above valley level, leaving only a thin gaunt pinnacle of rock stretching skyward like a gnarled finger.

It was the sort of landmark which

Indians in other times would have used for signalling at distance. Chris was rather surprised to find that the moss and other green growths upon it suggested that no one had used it for a long time.

With four hours of daylight still to go and no suggestion of a plan for the future, Chris did what he could for his troubled roan and settled back in his rock cover to await the passing of time. He felt quite anxious, but not desperate.

* * *

The man who crawled along to Chris' position some thirty minutes after total darkness had blackened his face and exchanged his army boots for a pair of soft leather mocassins. He had a pack on his back containing extra food rations and sufficient interest in the beleaguered man not to give away his position prematurely.

Chris was dozing in spite of his desire

to stay awake and he heard nothing of the stealthy approach until a faint whistle put him on the alert. The sound had come from behind him, from a totally unexpected direction. He did not know what to make of the situation until a pair of slightly breathless lungs, striving for near silence on grounds of security, provided the power for an old army marching tune which Bart Morgan had learned to play on a tin whistle as a boy.

Chris licked his lips and gave a few bars of his own version of the tune and within a minute the brothers were gripping one another's hands and chuckling with relief.

Bart produced biscuits and a canteen of cool water. The exchanges began at once, while they were still partaking of the scratch meal. Chris told everything he knew about the geography of the stronghold's approaches and spoke with foreboding about the cost in lives if such a small unit of the cavalry attempted to force an entry.

Bart chuckled. 'We ain't alone. There's a whole troop operatin' in these parts under the leadership of Captain Gray, an' you know what that means!'

Chris murmured with interest. Phil Gray was a specialist in rough going, the sort of officer who showed at his best when the geography happened to be against the army's best interests.

'You think Captain Gray will have a crack at gettin' into the stronghold from some other direction?' Chris wondered.

'Sure. He's studied all available maps of the region an' consulted a couple of geologists. He has with him a score of mules, climbin' equipment and some long heavy tracks made out of thick rope-weave for crossin' soft ground!'

Chris was vitally interested in these last revelations, but a few seconds of conjecture made him doubtful, even then, of Captain Gray's chances of success.

'If the captain gets his men fouled up in this land of bog and rock to the north of here, he might be court-martialled.'

'That's so, Chris,' Bart murmured, 'but if he succeeds where others have failed he could get accelerated promotion through to Colonel, and you know how ambitious he is!'

'What is Stride doin' right now?' Chris asked this question in an effort to mentally sidestep his own pessimism.

'He's holdin' his men in readiness to attack the mesa, an' at the same time acceptin' delivery of some extra items from the other detail further north.'

'It could prove suicidal to bring men along this *arroyo* unsupported by artillery,' Chris pointed out bluntly.

'The risk is not yours,' Bart chided him gently. 'Why not tell me about your own future movements an' then allow the army to take care of its own?'

Chris poured out his words in a torrent. They sounded good, but Bart knew him well enough to know that he had very little confidence in his ability to exploit the unknown alone. The corporal was also shrewd enough to know that his brother was troubled about the fate of Nerena Lester, believed to be in a position of extreme danger.

A few minutes short of midnight the brothers were on the move. Chris left the cover of rocks and sprawled down into the *arroyo* trailing a long head rope behind him. Up on the mesa, smoke and occasional flickers of flame suggested a guard keeping himself warm and alert.

Nobody challenged the crawling man, however, and he tugged gently on the rope to indicate that he was ready for the roan to attempt the same. Bart, still among the rocks, slowly released the horse and coaxed it to go after its master.

Whinnying quietly, the stockingfoot broke cover, struck a single shower of sparks off a rock with one shoe and at once plunged over the rim and into the stream bed. Chris whistled softly as it stretched its neck and nuzzled his shoulder. He issued a low command to the animal and crawled on ahead, not pausing until he was out of the gorge and up the other side.

The roan joined him without incident. Across the stretch of darkness the brothers faced each other, the one reading the thoughts of the other and wondering about the outcome of this exacting sortie against odds.

Chris was taking the initiative again. He had his knowledge of cavalry signalling to help him if the opportunity should crop up, but he was heading into the unknown and no amount of care, experience and courage could render him proof against the enemy's potential.

10

Chris used the remaining hours of darkness to good effect. Stalking along on foot in the mocassins of an old Indian scout who had once served Fort Comanche, he worked his way through the seemingly endless cluster of rocks and rimrock which populated the earth to the south of the mesa and close under its cliff on that side.

On one occasion a guard tossed an empty bean can over the edge and so startled horse and man that they almost gave away their presence.

Using his knowledge of the stars, Chris edged around the base of the mesa until he stumbled upon a worn track which was obviously the one used by such men as Dollar and Breeze who knew the entry routine. He maintained his vigilance and even risked mounting up when his venture was a little over two hours old.

It was dark on the west slope of the tableland and any amount of probing with the naked eye failed to reveal the path which led from bottom to top. Chris' shoulders were drooping and the roan was well past its best when a startled jackrabbit drew attention to the gap between two thick high bushes of buckthorn.

The roan recovered before Chris did. Something prompted him to pause at that spot. Between the two bushes he found a wooden marker post driven into the earth. Roughly gouged out of the top of it was a skull and crossbones. It took less than a minute to confirm that this was the bottom of the mesa guards' access track.

The discovery started Chris thinking again. Had Dollar gone up there to tangle again with his enemies, the Breezes? Or had he by-passed the lookout spot and gone on up the narrow track which led north to the inner workings of the renegade citadel?

He felt reasonably certain that Dollar was ahead of him. The cunning killer had every reason to get to the head man of the fortress before Long Tom Breeze so that he could give his version of recent events first. Dollar was a glib liar, but Breeze had four other men to back up his deliberations, should they differ from Dollar's account.

So Dollar was most likely further north. But what about those men up there? Already the eastern sky was streaked with grey. Very soon the lookouts on their flat-topped eyrie would be back in business again and anyone approaching would be vulnerable.

Was it worth it, Chris wondered, for him to mount a one-man attack up that animal track, in the hope of taking them by surprise around dawn? He knew that he was tired and in need of rest, and that the actual ascent would be tricky and somewhat unpredictable as to timing, and that if he succeeded in reaching the crest undetected the odds were still against him.

Abruptly, he abandoned the idea and mounted up again. While the sky was still relatively dark he wanted to make a lot of headway across Colonel Clervaux's territory. Storming the heights, he decided, was a job for the army.

He pressed on, using a narrow but very definite track which led in the direction hinted at by Dollar earlier. As he rode, he found himself wondering if the route had first been used by some huge grizzly bear or whether some blundering outlaw, running from the law, had fashioned and used it as the approach to his lair.

While streaks of bright light were still slowly cracking the darkness in the east he tied his brown leather vest more tightly around his chest, settled his stetson more firmly on his head and tightened his bandanna. After giving the roan a few gentle nudges with his knees, he set his body in the most restful position possible and slumped in the saddle for a light sleep.

With malice toward all, Dollar used the
few hours he had in hand to his best
advantage. He knew the lie of the land.
He by-passed the mesa, as Chris had
guessed he might. In failing to contact
the guards up above on the way in
Dollar had knowingly broken one of the
basic rules laid down by Clervaux.

Now, he sought to get himself as near
to the citadel proper as he could
without giving those who might seek to
follow him much assistance. He slept in
his blanket for three hours beside the
narrow track at a strategic point. Not
far beyond his selected camp, grey walls
of rock gradually mounted on either
hand, rendering the trail a narrow gap
between encroaching cliffs.

The defile persisted in this claustro-
phobic, scarcely-lit fashion for over a
mile. At that distance, a thirty yard gap
in a crosswise direction fell away into a
spume-ridden stream bridged only by a
wooden erection of vintage years, the

base boards of which were in need of replacing.

Beyond the gap and not far from the bridge's other extremity, a dark conical hole betokened the continuation of the defile in the same direction. On rising, about six o'clock in the morning, Dollar tightened his belt, fed his dun a few handfuls of the best grass in the vicinity and casually mounted up.

He had negotiated the defile before, but it never ceased to give him a feeling of foreboding which it was not easy to shake off. Long before the encroaching rocks shut out the daylight above him he was shuddering and cringing in the saddle and fumbling for something to give him confidence.

His searching hands rediscovered his lucky charm in a side pocket of his jacket. He rubbed the surface of it between finger and thumb, wondering how his complicated life would resolve itself on this trip. His throwing knife was once again strapped to his forearm, but the point was missing. Something would have to be done about that.

The semi-darkness swallowed him. Here and there on the rugged steep walls water dripped. Something hit his hat. It turned out to be bird droppings. In spite of himself he shuddered and coaxed the dun to greater efforts. By the time the defile opened out for the bridge his upper trunk was rigid. The dampness was through to the marrow of his bones.

Two fluttering bats came out of the cliffs as he emerged. They circled his head, so that he ducked to avoid them. When the dun slipped on a moss-covered stone he had to make an effort to get back to the problems of the immediate future.

He expected to be followed. Next along the track behind him would be Long Tom Breeze or one of his gang. Or there could be an outsider, Chris Morgan. Whoever came along there, Dollar had nothing to gain from contact.

As the dun stepped cautiously across

the worn planks of the bridge, Jake decided to do something to delay any sort of pursuit. He would demolish the bridge. Contemplation of the calculated act of destruction began to make him feel better. He chuckled, a rare thing for him to do on an empty stomach. Soon, he had dismounted. There was no necessity to peg out the horse as it did not relish the dark hole which was the mouth of the north end of the defile.

Using what tools he had, Dollar sawed his way through some of the platted ropes. He then worked on the planks with his boots and the stock of his rifle until the whole of the bridge on his side was ready to part company with the bank. After that, it was only a matter of leverage. A few robust heaves saw the planking on its way. It fell with a sudden crash into the foaming waters below, leaving only one or two shattered splinters dangling from the side opposite and a frayed rope.

For upwards of a minute, the wrecker stood by the edge of the bank looking down into the waters. A smile formed on his lips: that developed into a broad grin, and presently he threw back his head and indulged himself in a bout of gusty, raucous laughter.

Shortly after that, he removed his knife from his sleeve and bent down to work on the blunted point. The repointing of the weapon was not easy. It required concentration, and that calmed him down.

*   *   *

Two hours after Dollar demolished the bridge, Chris Morgan's nervous stockingfoot had roused its master and carried him most of the way through the southern end of the defile which ended where the bridge had been.

The defile was narrow and winding. Consequently, it was possible for a stranger to ride relatively close to the bridge area without being aware of the sudden changes ahead. Not much light penetrated into the recesses.

Chris was into the last fifty yards of winding passageway when the nightmarish surprise in store for him first manifested itself. A bullet whined from surface to surface some two feet above his head, and presently two others followed. The clatter of hooves was suddenly drowned as the ricochets buzzed this way and that.

The roan threw up its forelegs and whinnied in terror as the shells came whistling out of the gloom. Chris found himself sliding over the animal's rump and falling precipitately towards the dank rock floor of the narrow way.

His head connected with a rock projection, sending other noises through his skull and to some extent dulling the sensations of imminent disaster.

11

The echoes continued to buffet the walls of the defile long after the magazine of bullets had penetrated it. Chris' head buzzed for quite a while before it cleared. After a time, he realised that the shooting had ceased and that he was controlling his frightened mount by hanging on to a stirrup. In addition to that, he was on his knees. His legs had taken some punishment due to the way he had landed but it did not appear that any bones were broken.

Very cautiously, he straightened up, felt himself over for breakages and strains and decided that he had been exceedingly lucky. Someone up in front, at a guess that evil genius, Dollar, had planned a most hair-raising ending for him. Somehow it had failed.

Chris had doubts as to whether the

shooting attack would be renewed. His first constructive effort was to back the roan some thirty yards into a place where it could be turned about with relative ease. At that spot, he did his best to calm the creature and looped the reins round a rock pinnacle which resembled a hook in the cliff wall.

Calling soothing words to the horse, which miraculously was uninjured, he went forward crouched low with his Winchester to hand and all his nerves and sinews straining against a possible further sneak attack. The very gradual improvement in the light above him warned him of the imminence of the defile's mouth and he went to earth and crawled the rest of the way in case of further ricochets.

None came. He waited nearly ten minutes with his eyes probing the area of the bridge and decided that the dark maw of the further stretch of defile was no longer occupied. He tested the concealing darkness on three successive occasions, tossing small boulders and pebbles into it at various angles. There was no reaction, not even by bats. After that, he straightened up and walked cautiously to the edge of rock and looked down.

The angry water, pouring past quite swiftly from right to left, was a sight which had him gasping for breath. Clearly, there was no easy way down the cliff on either side in order to cross the stream at water level. He began to see that the man ahead of him had positively interfered with his progress and possibly cut him off in an impossible region with the likelihood of enemies on either hand.

It was the sort of thing that Dollar would do without thinking too deeply. Only Dollar could conclude that anyone coming along after him was sure to be his enemy. But why had not the gunman waited until Chris emerged into the open? With the victim in full view he could have made sure of an easy kill with no danger to himself.

Was the villain ahead so much a prey

to his own impatience? Or was there some other reason for the premature attempt at an ambush? Chris shook his head and decided to put that bit of conjecture back for a while.

The bridge recently demolished had been built over a natural stone bridge which had long since fallen in. The gap between the natural stone projections was far too wide for any sort of a leap. The closeness of the encroaching walls further cramped the area.

Chris could only take one course of action. He had to get back through the approach defile so as to give himself scope for another probing ride. If he did not clear the defile before anyone followed along his trail he could be trapped quite easily. Viewing the situation at its blackest, anyone catching him between the cliff walls could end his life quite quickly as the man up ahead had come near to doing.

In the half light, it was hard to know how far the sun had travelled across the heavens. Chris knew, however, that he had to make full use of any time still at his disposal. With a conscious effort he turned his back on the watercourse and re-entered the defile, whistling to the horse which awaited him in the gloom.

Frightened as it was, it neighed a welcome and soon he was being carried back in the opposite direction at a reasonable pace. The mile he had to traverse to get back into the open seemed long drawn out: until the time of the sudden noise.

This time it came from quite a distance. As far as the mesa or beyond and the confining walls of the cliff distorted the sounds for a time and made it difficult to identify them. Crouched in the saddle, Chris raised a hand to his ear in an effort to hear better. In doing so, he discovered a light burn mark in the side of his stetson which he had not been aware of before. A ricochet had passed within an inch of his brain . . .

The buffeting sounds came in bursts. At last, the height of the cliff walls began to fall away. Rays of sunlight bounced briefly into what was left of the defile at a time when the lone rider had almost made up his mind about the new noises. He felt sure that he was hearing rapid gunfire. The sort put up by a gatling gun, a rapid-firing weapon invented by R. J. Gatling about twenty years earlier. The gatlings Chris had seen possessed no fewer than ten barrels and were capable of firing over a thousand shots a minute.

If he *was* hearing a gatling, and he was doubtful about it, who could be aiming it? Was it part of the renegades' defences located on top of the mesa, or did the army have it with them? In the event of the cavalry having brought it along, it would be of little use against Breeze's guards on account of the height of the mesa above the surrounding country. Unless it could be brought up under cover of darkness and rigged on a sufficiently high platform to make the mesa vulnerable.

There was one such place: a stone platform sided by a useful pinnacle of rock which could be used to moor the running tackle for hauling the parts of the gun aloft. But was it feasible? Could it have been done during the hours of darkness without the guards being aware of it?

Chris abandoned his speculation as the roan walked clear of the defile and he at once became aware of new sounds. Another rider was approaching him at speed, and the distance between them was negligible. This newcomer was scarcely likely to be an ally. More likely to be a messenger of some sort, heading for the inner recesses of the stronghold.

A man who would know an alternative route to the demolished bridge. This was a time for ambushing. Chris dismounted and glanced up at the shelving cliff above him.

★ ★ ★

On top of the mesa at that very same time, all was still. Three men had died during the previous few minutes. One horse was already dead, and a second one died as the only survivor on two legs, Long Tom himself, shakily pushed himself to his feet and wondered at the devastation caused by that mighty multi-barrelled weapon which had been installed during the dark hours of the previous night.

In his whole life he had never known such carnage, such devastation in so short a time. Colorado had been almost cut in half across the chest as the flying bullets stitched him. Bummer Gorten had lost part of his crown, while Ringo, who had been on the move looking for firewood, had collapsed in a pool of his own blood.

The two Breezes had been the only ones to survive the sudden onslaught. Nate had slept to the rear of the grassed area and, consequently, he had been the lucky one when the curtain of bullets came across at them.

The group's riding horses had been pegged out in a hollow directly opposite the approach *arroyo*. Spraying bullets had accounted for a pinto and a claybank, but the horses' bodies had provided protection for the gang leader who had escaped with two small grooves.

Nate had been acting up a little of late, not getting on with his older brother. As a direct result of this, his was the only horse not in the forefront of the gatling attack and he was the furthest away from the storm of bullets.

Tom had shouted above the din of the firing, telling Nate to get down off the mesa and report to the main camp without loss of time. Most of his shouted instructions had been drowned out, but Nate knew what he wanted to do as he saw vividly the way in which his fellow riders died. He had grabbed his saddle and leapt for the skewbald's back, aiming to make the descent off the tableland before pausing to saddle up. His wild ride had paid off.

Tom saw him pull up at the foot of the mesa long enough to fix his blanket and saddle and then he had been off without a backward glance to report on the first great setback since the hideout was located. Tom sighed after his brother, feeling inwardly that they would not meet again and regretting the harshness he had meted out to him on the recent occasions when he had shown spirit.

Tom crawled away from the scene of the massacre on his belly. He felt that the army had the edge on him, that someone or another would scale the heights and eliminate him, even though he was prepared to sell his life dearly.

There was not much of interest for him to do. He glanced round about him and remembered that his horse, the finely-muscled grey stallion had somehow broken loose when the shooting started. He went after it, wondering if he would ever be in a position to put it to good use again.

In the saddle pockets he discovered

the well-matched pair of guns belonging to Crossdraw Willard Lester. They were guns to treasure, but at this time Breeze had no feeling for them. Ever since he had crossed trails with Jake Dollar things had gone from bad to worse. Now, he supposed, he could use the late federal marshal's weapons to defend himself. Maybe they would still claim a victim or two when the final clash on the mesa took place.

* * *

The final clash was due sooner than he had thought.

Inspired by the knowledge of his brother's need for support, Corporal Bart Morgan had played a big part in the first climb to the natural gun platform. He had been the one to swarm up and hitch the ropes and pulleys to the pinnacle of rock. Long before the rest of the crew had hoisted up the weapon's parts and assembled them, he had returned to valley level and conferred with Lieutenant Stride as to his future movements. So busy had the troops been in their clandestine task that no one had noticed Chris Morgan's covert moves earlier in the night.

Bart had left the rest of his detail on horseback and attempted to follow up the ill-marked secret trail which led around the south-west side of the mesa walls. Here and there, he had managed to pick out tiny marks left by horses which had passed previously.

Nearing the spot where the path snaked up the mesa side, his eyes tired of the prolonged staring and he failed to find the bottom of the ascent path. Consequently, he had hidden his mount among shrubs and scrub at the lower level and patiently awaited developments.

The gatling onslaught had surprised him although he knew it was planned, and the sudden appearance of the bulky outlaw, riding bareback, had surprised him still further. He toyed with the idea of shooting this fugitive from cover as soon as he had seen where the path came out, but before the younger Breeze reached the lower level the noise of battle ceased and Bart changed his mind.

Instead, he kept quiet, but crept forward on foot with his service revolver and rifle to hand. While Nate was hurriedly fixing his blanket and saddle, Bart moved to within fifty yards of him. And then the fair-haired red-faced outlaw was on his way. It seemed strange that the rider never looked back; never showed any further interest in the goings on on the high ground.

Bart shrugged, set himself at the formidable hill slope and started up it. It was a punishing climb for a man in ordinary trooper's dress. The mocassins he had worn earlier helped. Otherwise, he lost a lot of energy on the way up. As he struggled, his mind was busy with conjecture about how many men were still alive on the top. Chris had suggested five outlaws in all, before they parted on the previous day. One had ridden away. That left four. But were the four in a position to defend themselves, or had they succumbed to the deadly fire of the multi-barrelled gun?

The lack of sound from the top seemed to suggest no opposition, but a man in Bart's position could not take chances.

At the top of the slope, he had to lie down behind screening rimrock to regain his breath. While his cheek was still pressed to the earth he heard the unmistakable sounds of a man on the move. There was just time to shift his position a little further from the edge.

In the meantime, Long Tom had mounted up and was coming towards him. Marshal Lester's revolvers were pushed into his waist belt in the crossdraw position. Sharply in contrast to his younger brother, Long Tom frequently looked back. His restlessness enabled Bart to get into position behind a useful screening rock four feet in height.

The corporal awaited the approach of the rider with his rifle barrel resting on the top of the rock.

'That's about far enough, outlaw!'

The curt, decisive voice alerted Breeze in a flash. He checked the big grey, hesitated for a second in going for his weapons and finally attempted to crossdraw Lester's guns. Lack of practice in the late lawman's technique killed his usual speed long enough for Bart's first bullet to crash into his chest, and he slipped from the saddle gripping the matched revolvers with his arms still partially folded.

Bart moved up on him with caution as the riderless grey sidestepped him and pointed the rifle at the still figure from a distance of a few feet. The startled look was still on Breeze's face in death. Bart studied the athletic form, the flat features enhanced by the small ginger beard and the yellow bandanna finely contrasted with the dusty black riding outfit.

The subsequent survey of the defensive knoll took time and produced no surprises. Only two horses had survived the onslaught, and after five minutes Bart was able to hoist his hat on the end of his rifle and wave a signal to the squad manning the gatling.

He then moved into the hollow where the horses had been pegged and called out an explanation of the state of affairs around him.

12

In dropping from fifteen feet directly on to Nate Breeze and his moving horse, Chris knocked the wind out of himself as well as his victim. He had positioned himself where the rock sloped up at the entrance to the defile. As the two bodies crashed to the ground the skewbald leapt forward in shock, but the dark forbidding entrance to the narrow way stopped it as nothing else would.

The younger Breeze had lost his hat and his senses by the time the back of his head hit the ground. Chris was slow to rise. He came to his knees first and slowly stood up, rubbing his ribs. A single rifle shot carried to them just as the flattened man was regaining consciousness.

He felt himself over, cautiously retrieved his stetson and noticed that his holsters were empty.

Chris remarked: 'Howdy. I figure you for the lucky one of your gang. The rest would be wiped out back there by the army's gatling gun. How does it feel to be the sole survivor?'

Chris talked to him from a standing position with a Colt .45 in his right hand.

'Are you aimin' to use that gun, or are you jest nervous?' Nate wanted to know.

'What does it matter how I feel? I'm not pullin' the trigger yet. You can be of use to me, an' as long as the situation stays that way you go on breathin'. I want to get into the hideout. You can show me the way. Dollar has cut down the bridge through there, so you have to find an alternative route. Think that will be difficult?'

Nate rubbed his red cheeks thoughtfully and declined to answer in a hurry. He caught the water canteen which was tossed to him and studied the man who had the drop on him while he slaked his thirst. He took his time about the operation in an attempt to size up Chris's control.

'Did you say that was a *gatling* gun back there? How come you know so much about it?'

'It was a gatling gun, an' I know about such things because I was in the army myself until a short time ago. Now, what about this alternative route?'

Nate wanted to know what Chris' special interest was in the hideout, and to give him something to think about, the sandy-haired young man told him it was Jake Dollar. He also admitted to having fired on the Breeze outfit when they had Dollar staked out because he thought it was good for Nate to believe that he would not hesitate to shoot again, if necessary.

Some ten minutes later, Nate took the lead, heading away from the defile and threading his way just clear of rimrock as he skirted the foot of the giant upthrust outcropping in an effort to get back to the water-course further downstream.

This manoeuvre took upwards of an hour, but it looked to be worth while when they reached the banks again because the waters were not moving quite so swiftly and the banks were of soil and only a mere foot or two above the surface.

'What direction is the stronghold from this point?'

Nate glowered at Chris, and as he was not very good about compass directions and maps he merely pointed with his right hand. The direction he indicated suggested as near as Chris could judge north-north-east. That fitted in with what he had already learned. After receiving this approximate confirmation, Chris grew impatient. Breeze wanted a chance to eat. It was denied him until they were on the other side of the river. Nate was not a very good performer in water. His wariness of it showed up as soon as he put his skewbald down the slope. Chris noted it and decided that he was not likely to plan any treachery at the water crossing.

One after the other, the horses entered the water and were at once drawn downstream. The pace of the current was reduced but still formidable. The stream which had accepted them was in no hurry to give them up. They had done well to slacken their girth straps before taking the plunge.

Chris began to work the roan across the current, foot by foot. It was used to this work in water and it responded to his direction. Breeze and the skewbald did not have the same experience in water crossings. Nate began to jerk the animal's neck as Chris slowed up his progress. In an effort to bring its head round towards the far bank, the outlaw lost his balance and slipped sideways into the water. He cried out in alarm and Chris wondered for a few moments what to do for the best.

Breeze surfaced hanging on to a stirrup. He managed to hang on like that but could not regain his saddle. Chris deliberately lost a few feet of headway and managed to grab the skewbald's trailing reins. Almost five minutes elapsed before the roan managed to get a firm foothold on the other side.

Chris dismounted quickly so as not to be unsaddled. With his help the second horse made the bank and Breeze scrambled up beside it on hands and knees.

While the outlaw removed most of his clothing and saw to his personal comforts, Chris gathered kindling wood for a fire and set up the coffee pot. Breeze's inner needs prompted him to help and soon they were breakfasting off bacon and biscuits washed down by scalding black coffee.

A thick expanse of rough uneven ground, liberally strewn with stunted trees to the north of them ran wide of the regular route. Chris took the lead over this unmarked tract and kept going by instinct until late in the afternoon. At times when he slowed down he was able to read Breeze's thoughts by the way he looked around him.

Eventually, they blundered across the other trail and there they stopped to freshen up the horses. When they resumed Breeze was in the lead. After so many hours in the saddle, the red-faced outlaw was glad to talk for a while.

He revealed that the actual hideout was located in a canyon, thought by most of the men who used it to be a box. The entrance faced towards the east and was well guarded. It did, however, have a second means of access, a tunnel which had been fashioned by a stream in some earlier age.

It was to this tunnel that the track they were using led.

Within an hour their track converged with the climbing walls of the canyon to the east of them. Many small plants and hanging lianas clothed the steep slope, camouflaging the rocky structure in a sheen of green.

'Is the tunnel entrance gettin' close?'

Chris queried, as Breeze slowed in front of him and made a study of the slope.

Breeze grunted and declined to answer, keeping his back to Chris until the latter clicked the hammer of his Colt. That brought a response.

'As far as I can remember we have about fifteen minutes' ride to the entrance. I'm not very good at geography, though. It could be ten minutes, or even twenty.'

In spite of the casualness of the outlaw, Chris felt sure that if anything the opening was nearer rather than further away.

'I sure do hope you ain't worryin' yourself about trigger-happy lookouts, Breeze. Remember that Dollar has gone through and that he will have told them that the bridge is down. No bridge, no lookout, I guess.'

Breeze thought over Chris' reasoning, taking his time over it. Apparently, he came round to thinking the same. Although he was still anxious to pinpoint a lookout spot which was difficult to locate, some of the tension appeared to go out of him.

Chris, who decided purely on instinct that the opposition might be in readiness, slipped his Winchester out of the scabbard under his leg and held it across his body. He had no conscience about possibly sacrificing the outlaw but he had no intention of becoming a victim himself at this late stage of the approach.

Five minutes crawled by. The gradient had changed so that they were going down hill and speeding up a little. It seemed that Nate Breeze's thoughts were on what was to follow inside the stronghold rather than on the guard's challenge which he had expected.

Chris pulled the roan aside to avoid a boulder. At the same time, he glanced up at the slope. His attention was first taken by two squawking jays, seemingly disturbed by something, or carrying on a private feud. Some five yards to one side of them, where long grass and fern spilled over the front of a long grey rock, sunlight caught a metal object.

Before he could properly react, a rifle sounded off. For some reason best known to himself, Nate Breeze half raised his right hand. It might have been intended as a signal of some sort. Whatever it was, it was too late. The bullet ploughed through the base of his skull and sent him sprawling out of the saddle.

Chris' reactions were much quicker. As the head and shoulders of the outlaw guard appeared above the rock, he swung up the Winchester took a quick sighting upon the man's visible trunk and squeezed the trigger.

As Breeze hit the ground, his empty guns spilling wide of him, the man on the heights absorbed the bullet, temporarily disappeared from view and then stood up, showing himself to Chris down below. He twisted in the air as his legs buckled and fell on his back across the rim of the rock.

A grey stetson planed through the air, but Chris did not stay long enough to watch it land. He rowelled the roan and headed it down the slope, converging with the greater slope of the canyon's outer wall and looking for the opening in its side.

Only once did he look back. That was to satisfy himself that no other guard had witnessed the recent exchanges. He saw no one and from that moment forward all his faculties were used to discover the entrance.

Behind him, the riderless skewbald thundered at a gallop into a patch of scrub oak, until a branch caught the trailing reins and promptly arrested its progress.

Chris rode watchfully for another two or three minutes. The rock surface in the wall bulked out towards him. Trailing from the rock face was a profusion of hanging plants which did much to conceal the dark natural arch. But the roan, keeping to the ill-defined route, headed straight for the spot and Chris knew beyond any doubt that he had discovered the way in.

13

Colonel Herman Clervaux's settlement was indeed located in a canyon and as far as the regular outlaw visitors to the hideout knew, the canyon was a box. In other words, there was supposed to be no way out at the broadened nether end which faced westward towards the higher bulking backbone of the Rockies.

The Colonel's house was a separate residence built like a Spanish hacienda at the western end, beyond all the other buildings used by the permanent garrison and the visiting renegades. Around the time of this action, Colonel Clervaux was out of the habit of personally haranguing his guards and visitors. He stayed tucked away, aloof some said, and was content to relay his orders through his second-in-command, one Frenchy Lafitte.

A good hundred yards or more separated the hacienda from the nearest of the other buildings, which was used by Frenchy as his private office and quarters. Casually built in two lines were board buildings stretching still further towards the east and the canyon's natural mouth. These were the bunkhouses allocated to casual visitors, and sometimes used by resident guards.

Resident at this time were no less than three visiting renegade groups, Frisco James was the leader who came in last. The other two were Malachi Storme, a road agent widely known in Utah and Nevada, and Ricardo Velasquez, a fleshy Mexican who directed most of his illegal endeavours in the state of Texas.

Frisco James had reported to Frenchy the previous afternoon. He had radiated the new arrivals' customary good spirits, given up a percentage of his takings from recent robberies and relayed the information given to him by Long Tom Breeze at the time of the

193

Breeze gang's arrival on the mesa.

Over the evening meal, Lafitte, Storme and Velasquez had discussed the latest information and weighed it in some detail.

The discussion had warmed over the startling news of Federal Marshal Lester's death. There had been little discussion on the mesa, but Frisco had the opinion that the Breezes had accounted for Willie Lester and that they would have more to say when they were relieved of guard duty.

The strike against the stagecoach was only of passing interest, and the matter of United States cavalry manoeuvres in the area created no sort of a stir. Such things had happened before and nothing that the army had done had materially interfered with the day-to-day doings of the visiting renegades.

That morning, the gang leaders in residence had slept late, as was customary. After a leisurely breakfast, taken in Frenchy's quarters, they had strolled around the busy canyon, talking of their most recent exploits and discussing the current system of defences.

By mid-morning, they had tired of their walking and they returned with Frenchy to take coffee and share a few hands at cards. Some fifty yards away, many of the rank and file renegades — around thirty in number — were tossing horseshoes and gambling on the results of the game.

Malachi Storme, who was losing, had a thin film of perspiration round his left eye, which was hidden by a patch. Frisco and Frenchy were the ones with the true poker expressions. Ricardo Velasquez, the bulbous-cheeked Mexican, kept grinning open-mouthed, gusting tobacco breath through his yellowing gapped teeth.

By noon, the games were far more interesting and a slight atmosphere had developed in the room. A pause in the game was underlined earlier by Velasquez, whose ringed ears were particularly sensitive. He claimed that he had heard a distant noise, or a vibration of some sort, which boded ill.

The others all preyed on his superstitions, hoping that he would lose his flare for poker. To some extent, the Mexican's game did go off but it was not because of the unfair efforts of his fellow players.

The main though seldom used approach route to the canyon was on the east side. It came away from the rock and bog morass some miles to the east and sentries were placed at strategic intervals along its length, even though no forces of law and order had ever penetrated along that way.

It was from the eastern approach route that a mounted guard came into the hideout shortly after noon. Two rugged men on the permanent staff tried to dissuade him from approaching the hut where the leaders were taking their ease, but the fellow had been around sufficiently long to know that his information ought to be considered without delay.

Oddly enough, Velasquez, whose turn it was to play, was the first to look up and study the newcomer's face. The other three attempted to ignore the introduction, but the Mexican refused to make his move. His facial expression was totally relaxed. He awaited the information. Lafitte's brown eyes smouldered at this seeming interference with his authority. He hurled aside his undented brown stetson and ran the fingers of his free hand through the brown widow's peak of hair which grew low on his forehead. His neat brown beard and moustache bristled.

'All right, Jonas, why don't you say what you have in mind? You've interrupted this game, an' that's for sure.'

Wrinkles came and went in the weathered skin of the veteran Texan who had intruded. He took off his hat and toyed with it while he thought of the words to describe what he had heard.

'I'm real sorry, Frenchy, but you did

197

say when you gave me this regular sentry spot half way down the main approach that I was to get in touch with you personally if I thought anything important was developin'. Anything affectin' the security of the hideout, I mean.'

Frenchy lost his touchiness and at the same time was keyed up by the implications of his messenger's words. 'All right, Jonas, so you did right. Take the weight offen your feet an' tell it.'

The guard did as he was told, making use of a three-legged stool the seat of which was ample area for his narrow posterior.

'Around eleven-fifteen there was a curiously heavy noise came from the direction of the mesa. Kind of heavy an' concentrated. Hard to describe.'

'Could it have been a land slip?' Storme prompted.

Jonas shook his head. 'No, not that sort of noise. It's years since I figured in the army, but I would have said that it was some sort of new-fangled weapon.

Something on a big scale. A sort of field gun that fired a lot of small cartridges in quick succession. Not shells, but something along the lines of rifle bullets.'

'You don't have anything like that up on the mesa,' James said matter of factly, fingering his facial scar.

'Did you have any sort of signal from the direction of the mesa?' Frenchy asked.

As second in charge of the hideout, with a lot of authority delegated to him, Lafitte was more concerned than he was prepared to show.

'No signals, Frenchy. No signals at all. Jest this almighty blastin' noise which looked to be fired from east or south-east of the mesa against the guards on top. After that, nothin'. Did I do right in leavin' my post to tell you this?'

'You surely did, Jonas,' Frenchy replied warmly. 'Have yourself a couple of beers before you return, an' pass the word to other sentries up your way to keep a special lookout an' report directly anything out of the ordinary.'

The uneasy messenger beamed and withdrew. Frenchy stood up and paced about a bit. He sent another man round all the guards located near the canyon itself and then returned to the game and endeavoured to put some interest back into it.

At a few minutes before two in the afternoon, Velasquez had started to take the initiative again, after a few losing hands. Storme and James were acting like they were very hungry, hoping that Frenchy would curtail the session and break the Mexican's concentration.

A second interruption made Frenchy's intervention unnecessary. The door opened abruptly and a limping man who did many of Frenchy's messages stumped inside and whispered into his ear.

Lafitte's fine brows shot up his forehead. 'Jake Dollar has arrived? On his own? Are you sure?'

'Sure I'm sure, Frenchy. He came in

by the tunnel a short while ago an' he expected to be allowed to come right on in here like he was a gang boss, on account of him workin' on his own!'

Storme's face crimsoned. He pulled his eye-patch away from his face and let it go again. 'Two of my boys claim to have been swindled by Dollar over the proceeds of robberies in California. I'd like for to get my hands on him. It would be more interestin' than playin' cards.'

Ignoring Storme's anger, Frenchy went on: 'What did he have to say?'

Limpy shrugged. 'He was full of his own importance, like always. Says he killed Crossdraw Lester in Silver City, an' various other things. I think maybe it wouldn't be a bad thing to see him real soon.'

Frenchy went thoughtful over the lame man's advice. He flicked his brows in the direction of the other players and they agreed to postpone their meal until they had listened to what the latest arrival had to say. Dollar appeared in two minutes, his dark jacket and grey trousers being the worse for wear, and his derby hat set well back on his head at a jaunty angle.

He recognised everyone in the room, beamed at them and awaited their reply. When some of the steam had gone out of him, he was permitted to take a seat. He did this, and tossed forty dollars in notes on to the table, explaining that his last paid job had been a poor one.

'How come you're here an' not takin' a spell on the mesa, which you know is a rule of this establishment?'

Dollar chuckled and fingered his moustache. 'Because had I done so, Long Tom Breeze and his boys would no doubt have put a bullet through me. There's bad blood between us, so I by-passed the mesa, guessin' they were up there an' came straight on in.'

'Apart from savin' your own skin, what did you hope to achieve by comin' straight here? Do you have any special news for us? Anything to benefit the

Colonel's establishment?'

'In Silver City I put paid to the distinguished career of Crossdraw Willie Lester with my knife. I did that for two reasons. Firstly, I heard that he had sworn to take this hideout to pieces and eliminate every man who uses it. Secondly, I heard tell that the Colonel had placed a price on Lester's head. The figure I heard was two thousand dollars, payable on proof of the federal marshal's death. Am I right in my supposition?'

'Can you prove you killed Willard Lester?' Frenchy countered.

'Not at the moment, because the Breeze outfit stole the guns I was bringin' to prove my point, an' if an army unit hadn't sneaked up on their position when they had me pinned down, they would have shot me out of hand.'

Dollar, being an accomplished and habitual liar, thought nothing of missing Chris Morgan out of his narrative for the assimilation of his listeners.

'Are the Breezes in here yet?'

'Not yet. What do you know about an army unit operatin' near here?' Velasquez asked.

'U.S. cavalry, possibly on manoeuvres and possibly with a special assignment to carry out. A businesslike-lookin' lot who frightened the Breezes into backin' off when they were in a murderin' mood.'

The assembled gang leaders exchanged glances. All of them were concerned, but not unduly. Time would tell if their fears were groundless or otherwise.

'Did anyone follow you when you came along by the tunnel route?' James wondered.

'No, nobody.' Dollar grinned. 'It wouldn't have been at all easy because I cut down the old wooden bridge to stop the Breezes followin' me. Ain't that a laugh? Right now, you don't need to post a guard over the tunnel entrance because no one is comin' by that route any more.'

Frenchy cleared his throat. 'What do you know about sounds like heavy gunfire from the direction of the mesa towards midday?'

The bantering look slipped from Dollar's face. He looked mystified, for once, and clearly he was speaking the unadulterated truth when he replied.

'I didn't hear anything special around that time. Maybe it was because I was through the defile.'

Frenchy nodded. No one else had anything specific to ask. Limpy showed Dollar out of the room, on his way to one of the ordinary bunkhouses further east. For once, the slant-eyed man did not argue. He knew when not to push his luck and he had decided that this was one of those times.

★ ★ ★

The shooting near the tunnel entrance occurred between half past five and six o'clock in the evening. A group of men playing horseshoe tossing heard it and one of them dashed to the segundo's shack to give the alarm.

Frenchy sprang off his bunk in a flash and ran across the intervening space followed by Frisco James and Malachi Storme. Together, they toiled up the steep narrow winding track which led to the hole in the south wall of the canyon at an altitude of some seventy feet. The segundo was ahead by about ten yards when they negotiated the hole and came out on the rocky knoll which served as an elevated guard post for the tunnel entrance.

Frenchy gasped as he saw the position of the dead guard. Crouching low, he moved closer, his attention still upon the man he had personally sent up there at breakfast time. Storme and James came up on either side of Frenchy, breathing hard and likewise nonplussed by what they saw.

'Hondo Pierce,' Frenchy breathed. 'Outgunned by someone down below.'

Pierce was a homely-looking fellow.

His blue shirt was stretched tight over his barrel chest and stained with his blood. His eyes were open in death. The expression in the upside down face looked strange. A faint breeze was stirring the deceased's thin curly fringe around the bald crown.

James was already looking down below. 'Pierce's hat fell down when he was hit, an' the man who hit him is also dead down there. I saw him jest a few hours ago. That's the younger Breeze, name of Nate. He maybe came after Dollar seekin' some sort of revenge. What do you think?'

Storme said: 'Breeze must have known the signal. He was a fool if he failed to give it an' let Pierce shoot him.'

'If we can believe Dollar about the bridge, Breeze must have found another way round the creek,' Frenchy reasoned. 'He must also have lived long enough to get in a tellin' shot at the guard. I suppose we ought to send someone down there to collect Breeze and his mount.'

After dragging Pierce's body away from the overhanging rock, the thoughtful gang leaders returned to the buildings by the same route.

14

Around six in the evening, forty cavalry soldiers and artillerymen under the command of Captain Phil Gray were about to begin the assault on the last half mile of rock and bog ground a few miles east of the canyon. The troop had been working since dawn, and in the subsequent hours great use had been made of the twenty mules which came with the party.

Equally useful to the mixed unit were the stiff rope-weave mats which Gray used as tracks to prevent his men and materials from sinking into the softer parts of the boggy territory.

Grey was an intellectual who saw geographical difficulties as challenges. He had fought the unfriendly terrain all day, and had succeeded in crossing territory which no other military commander expected to be breached that century.

As a direct consequence, the robbers' roost was now definitely threatened for the first time in many years. Minus his tunic, Gray moved along the toiling line of his men, offering advice from time to time and not being afraid to curse the mules when they proved stubborn.

He pulled his mount to one side as a small team of men carrying the barrel of a light, dismantled field gun, staggered by. Although they were hard-pressed each man in turn contrived to get a glimpse of the officer who was making them do the impossible.

Gray looked tall in the saddle, and older than his thirty-eight years. His thin lined intellectual's face was rendered more distinctive by his black barred brows and the short straight moustache under his broad nose. His down-drooping mouth failed to show the elation he was feeling over this day's exploits.

Two bewhiskered old Mexicans had the distinction of being the regular guards located furthest from the stronghold, and it was during that last early evening struggle to negotiate the final half mile of unyielding territory that the lookouts noticed what was happening.

Pancho Garcia, seated on a grassy knoll above soil which had a fair quantity of sand in it, was the first to spy what was happening. He talked with the spyglass to his eye, his attention on the east.

'Only last night, amigo, you sayin' that we would camp out here for the rest of our lives, settin' traps for jackrabbits an' other small creatures an' that one day the Colonel would forget us altogether.'

Garcia was a small man with a profusion of white hair on his head and a smart black moustache which belied his fifty-seven years. Under his black, decorated steeple hat, the eyes which he applied in succession to the lens of the spyglass were as keen as when he was a young man.

Jose Sanchez was around the same age, but very different in appearance. He was of medium height and very fat, holding in his belly with a broad tooled belt. When Garcia addressed him on this occasion, he was kneeling on lower ground shaping a small wooden dagger. Sanchez sniffed and looked up, fixing his friend with his bulbous, eroded eyes.

'What have you seen that is goin' to prove me wrong, ill-begotten one?'

'A whole company of Yankee soldiers. Horses, mules, guns and all the things needed to blow the Colonel out of his private hideaway!'

Sanchez gasped, cut his finger with his knife, cursed and staggered to his feet, glancing around for his own spyglass. Having failed to locate it he accepted the glass of his friend and did not give his bleeding hand another thought until he had verified everything Garcia had mentioned and one or two other items, equally of interest and likely to promote alarm.

'I put it to you, amigo. This is the time to fly for the border, if you should be so inclined,' Garcia suggested.

In a whisper, Sanchez replied, 'But we can't slip away now an' leave the Colonel uninformed. After all, he has fed us. He has kept us, an' it is rumoured that his health is far from good. We must do the job for which we are paid. Do it *pronto*!'

Sanchez trembled a little with fervour, and Garcia smiled. He had known how his friend would react to the outrageous suggestion. Side by side, they moved off to their camp and they packed all their equipment as speedily as possible.

★ ★ ★

Two hours later, the Mexican riding partners entered the canyon proper, having been screened and identified by the closer guards. They made their way past the buildings and approached

Frenchy's residence unimpeded by anyone.

A brief knock on the door and they were admitted. Seats and refreshments were brought for them. The assembled gang leaders brought their chairs nearer and awaited the latest intelligence, which they felt sure was going to be of a disturbing nature.

★   ★   ★

Jake Dollar's second interview with Frenchy Lafitte and the visiting gang leaders had led to nothing. Frenchy had categorically turned down Dollar's application for the two thousand dollars' reward for the elimination of Crossdraw Willie, and it was clear by their attitude that the gang leaders in residence had little time for him or his claims. As he had known earlier, the word had gone around about earlier acts of treachery on his part, and these particular gang bosses were very well informed.

Jake, however, was never downcast for long. He had known from the outset that he only had an outside chance of picking up the revenue for Willard Lester's murder. Even if he didn't get the money, he had at least won for himself a brief respite within these canyon walls, and nobody this far had been howling for his blood, or pointing to the hanging tree.

Dollar had noted Colonel Clervaux's non-appearance among his men and his guests. He had further noted that talk of the Colonel's illness was not a topic being talked about among the permanent guards. And that had to mean something. If the Colonel was indisposed, then he had been indisposed for some time. Long enough for his indisposition to be thought unremarkable.

Such thoughts as these had been mulling over in the loner's mind when the two veteran Mexicans arrived from the east. He noted the way in which they were received and treated by younger white American guards and he shared almost everyone else's notion that they had vital news to impart.

As he wanted the news quickly and at first hand, he used his wits to get close to the building without disturbing the inmates who, he felt sure, would be annoyed if he burst in upon the latest conference. Jake headed for the door with the jaunty air of someone who had been sent for.

Twenty yards away a thoughtful resident guard stopped him and warned him that the segundo and the visitors were already engaged. Dollar raised his brows, slowed his pace but kept on walking. He grinned back at the man who had questioned him.

'Shucks, brother, I jest thought of something real important that slipped my memory the last time Frenchy an' I were talkin'. Maybe I ought to wait till his present visitors have finished, but he'll be mighty keen to hear what I've got to say. Tell you what I'll do, I'll wait outside. Then I won't waste any time when he's finished with the Mexican guards, huh?'

The guard was not at all keen to allow him that close during a conference, but as he pulled up on the steps and sat down there, not making any attempt to interfere with those conferring, he was allowed that measure of freedom.

Inside, the Mexicans were taking it in turns to answer questions. All the voices of the visiting leaders were clearly audible. Garcia answered well, but Sanchez' voice was husky and it did not carry as well as that of his countryman.

Consequently, Dollar stood up again, appeared to be judging the direction of the faint breeze, and stepped around the corner to light a small cigar. Keeping clear of the windows, he moved slowly along the side, no longer observed by the guard, and listened hard.

The purport of the exchanges was relatively easy to follow. The messengers had clearly put it across that a big unit

217

of the army, backed up by mules and artillery, had succeeded in crossing the rugged bog and rock terrain to the east and that within a few hours they would be in a position to threaten the inner resources of the canyon itself.

Every question asked them confirmed the menace rather than diminished it. Dollar, on the outside and hearing with ease, wanted to whistle, but he contented himself with rocking his hat by pushing the brim at the nape of his neck against the wooden wall. For an encore, he sucked heavily upon his cigar and blew several smoke rings.

Quite soon after that, the type of questions changed. Few of the younger men in the garrison knew that Sanchez and Garcia had been officers on the other side in that earlier war between Texas and Mexico. Frenchy had learned sufficient of their background to ask their advice on delicate matters like basic strategy.

Some five minutes later, Frenchy

attempted to sum up their collective advice. 'So it comes to this. We can muster about thirty visiting guns and twenty guards. About fifty in all. The army could have anything up to sixty men against us, backed up by horses, mules and field guns. Other things bein' equal, they could take us apart.

'So what do we have to do for the best? Either we slip out and meet them on the main approach track, fighting a delayin' action before movin' away either to north or south, or we dig ourselves in here to the best of our ability an' use a fair amount of dynamite to neutralise the army's advantage.'

No one envisaged slipping away without offering a fight, and all present agreed with Frenchy's summing up of the situation. There was the sound of chairs being moved, and that was the signal for Jake Dollar to saunter off round the other end of the building while he weighed up what he had overheard.

Once again, his allegiance to the outlaws was a fleeting notion of little substance. They had denied him his just reward for killing one of their bitterest enemies and that was all the excuse he needed to consider only himself from that moment on. After all, any man who put others before number one, himself, was a fool according to Dollar's philosophy.

He started to think into the future.

In the event of battle being carried all the way into the stronghold and the army coming out on top, every villain would be treated on his merits. Anyone doing the army a favour might also do himself a favour at the same time.

Thinking with the mind of an experienced assassin, it did not take long to arrive at the person most likely to top the army's list of wanted men. None other than Colonel Herman Clervaux could aspire to that exalted position. Clervaux, who had been disgruntled and out of touch with law and order since the early days after the civil war when the Yankees had taken advantage of the defeated south.

If Jake could eliminate the head man of this whole concern, or ensure that he fell into the hands of the advancing army units instead of escaping, then that would be something to aim at. Having arrived at that conclusion he stepped clear of the building largely used by the segundo and casually began to study the distant hacienda with the unusual turret on its roof.

15

Towards eleven o'clock, Chris Morgan, who was becoming tense with inaction and frustration, decided that it was time for him to make a positive move. In traversing the tunnel, three hours earlier, his luck had held. The growing light had shown him where the opening lay ahead.

The ancient stream, long since dried out, which had created the tunnel, turned abruptly to the left and followed the cliff on the south side of the canyon floor. Anyone using that means of access usually walked or rode out of the arroyo and turned right.

Chris had purposely turned left, keeping to the gorge and using it for cover. Further into the canyon and mostly towards the right, there was much activity among the occupied buildings. Mindful that he had to stay out of sight if he was to maintain his freedom, he dismounted and effectively brushed out the sign left by the roan and his own feet with his vest.

Having done that, he moved up about a hundred yards and slackened his saddle, doing what he could for his own creature comforts and that of his mount. Without darkness to protect and conceal he knew that he could achieve little.

As early darkness greyed the inner end of the canyon, he had crept away from his hiding place and crawled far enough to have a good view of the isolated hacienda. Using his glass in the last of the fading daylight, he had studied the main building and decided that Colonel Clervaux had to be in there somewhere.

Only two humans revealed themselves to him. Both of them were slim, alert dark-skinned young men in black sombreros and ponchos of the same colour. They had useful-looking rifles and revolvers and knives showed around their waists. He thought they looked dark enough to have a touch of Indian blood mixed with the Mexican in their make-up.

These two occasionally moved around the back of the hacienda, but mostly they stayed in front, one at each side, and their attention was focused upon the other buildings and the men who came and went among them. Evidently, these two were the supremo's special guards and men not to be trifled with.

By their attitude, the uproar around the bunkhouse buildings suggested unusual happenings, perhaps an emergency of some sort. Perhaps twice in an hour, their steps came together and they conversed in low tones.

The turret on the flat roof had been specially built. It had substantial walling up to the height of a man's waist. Above that level, there were windows which appeared to slide back on runners. One of them was open. It could be used as a lookout tower, and in an emergency it would prove invaluable to keep off enemies.

Chris decided that he would have to out-fox the two Mexican guards by working his way round the back of the building and attempting to get closer to it from that side. He checked his weapons, did a few exercises which he had learned in the army to counteract his jumping nerves, and fixed his mocassins afresh.

Now that he was ready to go, he wanted something to spur him on his way. He was feeling more lonely than he had felt since starting out on his lone expedition. It was good to know that the army was in action and probably preparing a useful frontal assault, but that would avail him little if he was outsmarted in this remote neck of the canyon. He asked himself if it would not be better to lie low altogether and let the superior forces flush out the hideout in their own good time. But that he could not do. He felt that he had a special need to take a personal part in Colonel Clervaux's demise on account of what had happened to Crossdraw Willie, and because there was a chance that Nerena was somewhere here, within a few hundred yards of him, and in a situation fraught with danger.

He closed his eyes and conjured up a vision of Willie's niece, the desirable Nerena, whom he had only met on two or three occasions but who had shown more than a passing interest in himself.

Nerena ... A small and shapely brunette in her middle twenties, with shoulder-length shiny black hair. Green eyes in a broad face which showed a lot of intelligence and generated warmth to the whole human race. She wore simple, tunic-style dresses in bright colours which accentuated her becoming feminine bulges and added a touch of magic to the way in which she moved. He thought that in other circumstances she might have made a great dancer, but episodes early in her life had made her want to aid the sick and the weak, even though medicine was still looked upon in the United States as a man's profession.

Nerena. He found himself humming a catchy dance tune which the two of them had enjoyed when they came together at a dance in distant Fort Comanche. He found himself smiling. His future happiness lay with her. The memory of her offset his encroaching loneliness and gave him the impetus to start him on his way.

He left the scene of his camp and crept off with infinite caution. The nearer of the two guards, the one with the close-cropped turned-down black moustache and short beard, occasionally turned in his direction and appeared to be sniffing the air. It was almost as if he could sense an intruder. Any suspicions the guard felt, however, failed to lure him away from the front of the hacienda.

Chris crept on, his Winchester held firmly in one hand and his spyglass in the other.

Half an hour later, he was directly behind the house, on his knees and preparing to leave the gully for a neat path some three feet wide which led up to the rear door. It had been turned just recently and the soil was dark. His straining eyes could pick out two drain pipes coming down from the flat roof, one either side of the door. There was a faint light in the room to the right probably coming from a lamp turned down low. To the left, he occasionally saw shadows through a window. Shadows which could have come from a young woman plainly busy on late night chores.

He wondered if that could be Nerena herself, or was it some devoted Mexican servant woman, possibly a relation of the two tireless men guarding the front? A faint plume of smoke came out in wisps from a stove pipe located to one side of the turret. The windows to the left appeared to be on the steamy side.

He crept forward, aware of the weight

on his knees. His lower limbs protested at the work they were called upon to do in the interests of stealth. His lips constantly dried out. Half way to the house, he guessed what the woman was doing. She was taking a bath! From time to time he heard faint snatches of song. His straining ears pinned it down as a soldier's lament. The sort of sad song the army sang about a trooper returning from the wars to find everything he had fought for sadly changed.

Did that mean it was Nerena, singing a song she had picked up from the cavalry, or was it some other woman seeking to offset her loneliness by trilling words which meant little to her?

He felt he could not risk trying to make personal contact with the singer from outside. Apart from the faint noises from within, that part of the canyon was remarkably soundless. Further off, the guards and visitors seemed to be making a night of it. Something big was planned: something which would not wait until morning.

If the leader of the whole outfit was in the hacienda, surely sooner or later someone would approach the building seeking specific orders. In the event of a consultation taking place, Chris' position might become a little too tricky.

He wondered fleetingly how that other tricky person, Jake Dollar, was making out, and then his mind was made up. He would attempt to get close to the rear wall unnoticed and do his best to effect an entry by climbing one of the pipes to the turret above. He tried to size up what his chances were of completing the manoeuvre undetected, but that had the effect of rather putting him off. He had to make his move, and he had no time to waste.

16

In any other circumstances Jake Dollar would never have been given such freedom to move about on account of his unsavoury record over a long period. But this was an emergency, in which the garrison and visitors had little chance of coming out on top, and only a slim chance of getting away with their lives.

At nine o'clock, another guard from the main approach track reported that the army units which had crossed the bog and rock barricade were still steadily moving closer, with no sort of indication that they would slow up and dig in for the night. They were, in fact, almost within the range required for the light field guns to start peppering the mouth of the canyon.

This disconcerting news could not be kept from the ordinary gun fighters and road agents, who gathered together in their own small groups and talked about a fight to the death, or of splitting up and having it away through the tunnel before the artillery began to make itself felt.

Lafitte had long resented the old Colonel's absolute authority within the stronghold, but this was hardly the time to take over from him when the whole community was threatened with extinction. For the time being, Frenchy buried his ambitions and concentrated on making sure that the various groups stayed put and made themselves available for a concerted and all-out effort when the army came.

He still had a feeling that they could hold them off for one night. Any talk of withdrawal could wait until daylight.

Dollar kept away from those who knew him well. He hovered on the extremities of other groups, and did not attempt to draw away from the buildings until the light had totally gone and he had assimilated all possible information. He had sensed that relations between the supremo and the segundo had been strained for some time, and if anything went wrong with his latest efforts up at the house, he felt he could trade upon that knowledge to his advantage.

Getting past the two slim Mexicans was no easy task. Dollar was impatient. He had with him a good Spencer rifle, his usual pair of revolvers and his knife, now resharpened to a useful point. Working almost intuitively, he slipped into the *arroyo* which had earlier hidden his rival, and began to make sounds calculated to draw the nearer of the two Mexicans after him.

Two or three pebbles caused the guards to confer with one another. The nearer of the two, acting with extreme caution, began to edge his way nearer the gorge. He walked first a few yards in one direction and then zigzagged in another. Within ten minutes, he had a fairly shrewd idea that a man was hiding in the *arroyo*, and he could pinpoint his position within ten yards.

The nature of their job gave the young guards patience. This one, whose name happened to be Jimenez, still kept on the move so that the tricky one would find it difficult to shoot him, if that was what he intended to do. His partner, Lazaro, would start to stalk the position if he did not reappear in his customary patrolling area within ten minutes. A faint whistle was all that was necessary to bring Lazaro hastening to his aid.

Still on the move, Jimenez decided that he would whistle. He paused briefly for three or four seconds, lifting a finger and thumb to his lips. Had he known about the expert knife-thrower he might have hastened a little, or thrown himself to the ground. In seeking for absolute certainty in his aim, Dollar just gave him long enough to utter his faint whistle.

The throwing knife buried itself in his chest immediately afterwards and Jimenez slumped slowly to the ground, going down on his knees first. His body tilted forward and his steeple hat came off and rolled down the slope, ending up at Dollar's feet.

The assassin took that as a good omen. He picked up that hat, and on hands and knees, still moving with the maximum caution he ghosted back to his latest victim. Oddly enough, the hand which gripped the rifle still held it, which accounted for the comparatively silent kill.

Using the corpse first as a shield, Dollar peered around to see where the other guard was. He found that some forty yards separated them and that the other Mexican was weaving slightly on silent feet, heading for the arroyo at another point. It was fortunate that the moonlight lacked power so deep in the canyon.

Breathing quietly through his mouth, Dollar stripped the black poncho off his victim after first removing and wiping his knife. He took off his derby hat, an item which he was seldom without except in bed, and donned the poncho, following it up with the bigger brimmed headgear which sat upon his head rather tightly.

After rolling the dead guard into a slight depression on the bank of the gorge, he cautiously stood up and revealed his position to his partner. The other man stood still for a moment, clearly nonplussed by this latest move. Dollar shrugged in a pronounced fashion and waved the other back from the edge of the gorge. He hoped he was giving the impression that the emergency was over and that they should return to routine patrolling. Another wave brought a quicker response from Lazaro who began to think that his partner's nerves must have been affected by all the noise and hullabaloo further down canyon.

He began to walk back in the direction from which he had come, his movements indicating that he would come close to his fellow guard to exchange a few words on the way.

Dollar half sauntered towards the second man, holding the poncho up and away from his throwing arm with the shoulder weapon which he had firmly clutched in his left hand. Perspiration was starting out around the sweatband of the borrowed hat as the knifer waited for the maximum safe time before attempting to despatch another victim.

In spite of the tension, he was full of confidence. On this occasion, he made an upward throw of the weapon instead of bringing it from behind his shoulder. The darkness might have deceived him, or the Mexican might have ducked, but inevitably the guard was hit. He staggered and made vague snorting noises before Dollar came up with him and discovered that the knife was through his throat.

Jake extracted it as the poor fellow folded up, using his poncho to protect his arm from the spout of blood which followed. Glancing sharply around him, he lowered the Mexican to the ground and pretended to be administering to him. This was in case he was observed from the hacienda or elsewhere.

He studied the turret which was in darkness and decided that there was no one up there. He was breathing hard, but feeling very sure of himself as any assassin might do who had perpetrated two killings in a short space of time. At first, he thought he might drag the body of his second victim along to the house with the idea of asking for assistance, but he thought better of that ruse and decided instead to carry the guard to the edge of the *arroyo*.

That effort cost him a lot in energy and as he put the corpse down he hoped that it had been worth while. As soon as he judged that they were out of sight from the house, he used his leg as a lever and sent his victim rolling down the slope.

Following that manoeuvre he straightened up and considered the lie of the land. The nearer walls of two of the remote buildings were outlined in lamplight, but there was no sign of anyone coming up from there to visit the house.

The house itself was dark on one side and mildly lit up on the other. The dull glow suggested a lamp trimmed for night comfort rather than visibility. He did not consider that anyone could read by it, and his guess was that a sick person occupied the room; one who required a night light.

And some attention, which Jake himself intended to provide.

★   ★   ★

Chris' effort to get into the hacienda by way of the turret took him upwards of twenty minutes. As soon as he was in there, he felt weak. Even though the window by which he had entered was wide open, and another one on the opposite side was drawn back, he felt claustrophobia. A sense of being hemmed in.

For upwards of five minutes, he

stayed in the same position with his shoulder blades resting against one wall and his feet planted some eighteen inches apart. His mouth was wide open and he had great difficulty in breathing without give-away sounds. Perspiration coursed down his forehead, neck and face and before long a growing ache in his right arm reminded him that he still had his Winchester clutched in that hand.

He lowered it carefully into a corner and wondered how he had ever managed to negotiate the drain-pipe, the flat roof and the hard smooth walls of the turret without actually scraping the weapon noisily against one of the surfaces. As he contemplated the risks he had taken, perspiration spurted from him afresh.

He felt exhausted, and yet the peculiar position he had achieved would not allow him to relax for more than a moment or two. His first searching glances through the opened windows revealed no signs of the

Mexicans which he had been to such pains to by-pass, and for this he was relieved because there was something else much closer at hand which needed his attention with greater immediacy.

The singing had stopped long before he was up the drain-pipe, and he had no clear idea at first in which part of the building the woman was located.

The turret's other secret was bothering him now. It appeared to be built quite centrally over the one-storey house, with some sort of central passageway or hall directly beneath it. There was a trapdoor in the floor giving access to the supposed hall.

Also in the floor of the turret, and within a foot of its walls were openings, at least four inches in width and two feet in length. Their main use was more sinister than for ventilation. They were intended for observation and for gun slits. Anyone secreted in the turret, as he was, could look down into three of the four rooms below and immediately around the hall.

A source of intense frustration for Chris was the fact that the fourth had been deliberately blocked up with a length of timber. The fourth room was the one in which he suspected the woman of taking her bath. Seeing the bath and the bathing would have been a pleasant distraction for a man who had been on his own too long, but what mainly irked him was not being able to see who it was. He had no means of knowing whether the woman in question would turn out to be friend or foe.

Casting aside notions of wishful thinking, he decided that it was either Nerena Lester or most definitely a foe. He yawned and applied himself to the slit which gave out the faint light. Partly screened from him by the narrowness of the aperture was a large iron bed-stead.

Clearly it was occupied because he could see the shape of a pair of legs facing towards him. There was something rather other-worldly about the atmosphere in that room and it did not take long for him to discover why. The breathing of the bed's occupant was so feeble that it was undetectable from above.

He shifted his kneeling position and experimented, seeing how much more of the room he could see by lying in prone position. While he was still moving about he became aware of a long mirror located above a dressing table. Reflected in the mirror was the face of the man who had earlier been propped up in the bed.

A heavy quiff of grey hair hung forward over a heavily lined forehead. The eyes were closed in deeply eroded, lined sockets. Peering hard, Chris tried to assess the age of the bed's occupant. The skin of the face appeared to have a whitish pallor to it in the faint light of the lamp. Stretched out in that position, Colonel Herman Clervaux looked to be any age round about eighty. He had fought in the Mexican War, as well as the war between the north and the south, but the campaign which had taxed him the most was that fought against his own failing health.

A slight noise somewhere caused Chris to straighten up quickly. He straightened in his mocassins, noting the great activity around the distant buildings and then searching the nearer area for the elusive shadow-like sentries. He was reflecting to himself that he had not heard anyone in the vicinity of the house utter a single syllable to another human being when he caught sight of a moving figure.

One of the steeple hat brigade was coming from the nearest point on the *arroyo* rim and moving purposefully towards the house. This one came without hesitation, without pausing to look to right or left. A man with a purpose. Chris watched him, his eyes and his forehead only visible above the sill of the window on that side.

He was reminded of the early terrors of his boyhood. Things that went bump in the night and that sort of thing. He continued to watch, literally fascinated by the guard's stealthy approach. Why had he come all the way out of the *arroyo* with not so much as a sound, and no sign of his partner anywhere? Had he by some mischance become aware of his — Chris's — stealthy entry into the building? And what was his purpose at this time of the night? Was he bringing a message, perhaps something for the supremo's ears only? Or what?

Perhaps he had a secret assignation with the woman ... Chris brushed such considerations aside. Perhaps the fellow was not a guard at all, but someone masquerading as a guard. A steeple hat could change everything in that faint moonlight.

Chris switched off his thoughts and awaited the newcomer's entry. There was no time to think ahead now. The entry was almost entirely silent. Too silent even for a man who did not want to awaken a sleeper. It was the silence of stealth.

Chris drew his revolver from the

holster and slowly moved it up his body until he had it by his shoulder. Then he knelt again, beside the aperture above the supremo's bedroom. He wondered whether he should make some noise and risk the consequences, but the intruder moved so quickly he did not have the chance.

The door to the bedroom opened and closed. The mirror showed that a figure had entered. Almost entirely concealed by the black sombrero and poncho, the intruder held back and recovered his breath. There was no reaction at all from the man in the bed. Such stealth had nothing to do with the delivery of a message.

Chris began to feel more and more certain that he was about to witness the murder of the old Colonel by this silent fellow who was little more than an apparition. Inevitably, his thoughts raced back to Jake Dollar and his silent methods of killing. The knife, for instance.

Even as the hidden young man

entertained the idea the bedroom intruder folded back part of his poncho and revealed a knife comfortably held in the right hand. Mouthing the name of the assassin with whom he had been accidentally associated, Chris willed Dollar to move a little further into the room to permit a direct gun shot at him.

The killer stayed where he was. The act of slaying with the knife was a deadly efficient one, swiftly executed. Before Chris could so much as gasp the knife had entered the old man's chest directly over the heart. Chris gritted his teeth, still hoping against hope for a move of a foot or two from the assassin.

And then the totally unexpected happened.

Almost directly beneath Chris, in the doorway of the bedroom, the hammer of a revolver clicked. The single sound was sufficient to cause the assassin to leap further into the room, either to retrieve his favourite weapon or to be in a better position to use another. This action gave Chris his chance.

He aimed his revolver through the narrow aperture and pulled the trigger. In the interior of the house the explosion sounded rather loud. It drowned the cry of the woman standing in the doorway and also a noise less pleasant from the lips of the pseudo-Mexican.

Chris saw him slide to the ground, having been hit in the chest and he decided that this was the moment when he had to leave the turret and get below at all costs. He turned about, fumbled back the trapdoor and went down the steps at a speed which bordered on the reckless.

At the foot was the woman with the unfired gun. She had collected the lamp from the bedroom and she held it firmly until she was assured of the identity of the man coming down the open stairs. At last she sighed and her hand shook.

'Chris! Chris Morgan, if it hadn't

been you I don't know what I'd have done!'

'Pulled the trigger and shot whoever it was who had intruded from above, I shouldn't wonder, Nerena,' Chris returned hoarsely.

He grabbed the lamp from her, put it on a narrow table and clutched her in his arms. She was ready for all the warmth, affection and company that he could give her, having been in a state of tension for rather a long time. The softness and desirability of her was getting through to him, but pressing dangers made him shorten the embrace and look further into recent happenings.

Stepping between her and the man who had sunk to the floor, he moved into the room. She retired again and retrieved the lamp.

'The old man's dead, Nerena. I'm sorry I was so slow, but I couldn't get a sightin' on the killer until he moved after hearin' your gun click!'

'Don't worry about the Colonel. He

died while I was in the bath. I wouldn't have allowed this fellow to get so close if he'd still been alive. His heart gave out, that was all. It had been expected for weeks. That's what I was here for. To nurse him. There wasn't much else anyone could do, not even a first class doctor.'

The fallen man groaned. Chris turned him over, stripped the sombrero off his head and called for the lamp. Nerena came behind him with it.

'This is a man with several names. The one I've used for him is Jake Dollar. He has killed many times. Might have killed the Mexican guards. More important to us, he killed your uncle, I believe, in Silver City.'

Dollar was far gone, but he managed a wry chuckle, even in his fading state. Chris made sure he had no secret weapons near to hand and then put a spare pillow under his head. He felt sure that this ill-begotten assassin would have something to say before he expired, and he could just possibly divulge information which might be of use. Nerena had taken a seat, the better to recover from the shocking news.

'How did you get him away from town, Dollar?'

'In the red trunk which the senator mistook for his own. All would have been well, except that Lester gripped my lucky silver dollar when I knifed him and it went into the trunk. So I had to get it back . . . '

A thin trickle of blood seaped out of the corner of Dollar's mouth and seemed to suggest that his time was near. He coughed, reddened and won himself a brief respite. Glancing from one to the other of them, he wanted to say wounding things.

'You won't get away from here. The army has used a gatling already on the Breeze boys at the mesa, an' another detail has brought cannon an' mules across that boggy ground. But you won't get free. It's too late for the garrison to go out by the main approach an' fight the army there.'

'Why won't we get out, Jake?' Chris asked calmly.

'Because when the shells start knockin' hell out of the buildings an' the boys down there, they'll go berserk. They'll be down here an' shoot the pair of you when they can't find a way out! Mark my words!'

Dollar opened his mouth to say more, but his heart gave out at that instant. Chris lowered him to the floor and placed the sombrero over his face. In spite of the gravity of the situation, the sandy-haired young man had questions to ask of a personal nature.

'Did you have any idea it was me who dropped in through the turret?'

Nerena's strained expression eased. She put her hand briefly to the green hair band which made her look like a beautiful Indian maiden and stroked down the fringed buckskin dress she was wearing with nervous movements.

'I knew it was you because when you were climbing up the pipe you sang a few snatches of a song under your breath. I was jest the other side of the wall an' recognised it from way back. Another time when you sang it to me, after a dance. Do you remember?'

Chris nodded. He remembered only too well. What surprised him was that he had sung it unwittingly at a time when he was supposed to be maintaining absolute silence.

While they were standing in the hall just talking and looking at one another, the first of the shells from Captain Gray's artillery began to probe for the mouth of the canyon. At once there was a great outcry from the far buildings.

'There could be a lot of truth in what Dollar said before he died,' Chris pointed out.

Nerena danced up the stairs into the loft, where Chris joined her.

'Here they come now,' the girl breathed. 'That'll be Frenchy, the second in command, and the visitin' gang leaders. I think I'll have a shot at handlin' them. You go down there, make sure the front door is barred an' hand me up a rifle. All right?'

Chris marvelled that she was so composed, so clear-thinking on this night of nights when she had experienced killing already and heard without warning of her uncle's death. He concluded that she was a true Lester, all the way. He dashed down below to carry out her bidding. After securing the doors he turned his attention to the windows. By the time he had been in all the rooms, he was breathless again and unsure where to position himself.

Almost as an afterthought he went back into the supremo's bedroom and plucked the killing knife from his chest. He was no sooner out of sight than he heard a man approaching the house.

'I'm comin' right in, miss, because we need immediate and specific orders from the Colonel. Don't try to stop me.'

'Stay right where you are, Frenchy! The Colonel has already given his orders to me. He knows the state of affairs outside the canyon. In accordance with earlier instructions when you undertook to abide by his rule, he orders you and all the other men in the canyon now to make your exit by the main approach route!'

Another shell whined in through the mouth of the canyon and crashed into one of the bunkhouses, which folded up like a pack of cards and started to smoke.

'But it's too late to try an' fight our way out *that* way!' Malachi Storme protested.

'You wouldn't understand, mister, but the Colonel is an old military man an' his orders stand! You are to leave by the eastern route an' you can take those field guns away from the army by stealth if you've got the guts! You are not to concern yourselves about him or me, an' on no account are you to delay your advance, so I'll thank you to be on your way!'

There was a lot of dissatisfaction among the grouped leaders. Velasquez and James came up to the front of the house and attempted to peer into the Colonel's bedroom window. Up above, Nerena was still equal to the threat. She showed them the barrel of her rifle.

'Furthermore, if any of you act in an unmanly fashion, I'm authorised to speed your departure with this weapon!'

Storme and Lafitte stepped back hastily. Chris had to click the bolt of his Winchester a couple of times in the darkened bedroom to scare away the other two. Almost at once, however, Nerena reported that they were withdrawing. She came down the stairs again and opened the front door.

'In a little while, sheer terror over the shellin' might drive them back, Chris. We have to do what we can to discourage them from overrunnin' us like Dollar said!'

Two more shells at that moment plummeted into the canyon with devastating effect. Another building was shattered, and half a dozen men who had been dug in across the mouth of the canyon prepared to withstand infantry, lost their lives as the second shell pitched into their midst.

The cries that went up made the place sound like a battle field at night. Adding to the effect, the first building to be hit caught fire and started to burn rapidly. Crackling wood drowned some of the startled cries of the beleaguered outlaws.

'How do we discourage them, Nerena?' Chris asked breathlessly.

'By blowin' up the rock walls between them an' us with dynamite,' the girl explained.

She sent Chris down the *arroyo* where his horse was still located to find a rock with blue paint on the top. Underneath the rock, in a box, was a bundle of dynamite sticks attached to a long fuse. While she went surefootedly in the dark to the other side of the canyon, he searched for the hidden box, found it and placed the explosives directly under a series of spreading cracks in the cliff wall not very far from the tunnel entrance. While he worked, further shells from the deadly battery outside threw up craters which were illuminated by the spreading fires among the buildings.

Chris was paying out the long fuse to its fullest extent when there was a rush of men from the action area. One or two of them were mounted, but mostly they were on foot. With the end of the fuse in his hand, Chris threw himself down flat to avoid being seen.

He watched dry-mouthed as the fear-ridden outlaws poured into the tunnel in the hope of getting out of the canyon before the troopers and gunners of the main army group hemmed them in. Into the dark maw of the opening they rushed with only two flaming torches to help them.

As he fumbled with a match taken from his hat, Chris wondered if they stood a chance of getting clear, or whether Lieutenant Stride's men could possibly have located the secondary route. He struck the match and applied it to the fuse, watching it splutter and wondering how long it would take to get to the explosive. He also wondered how much of the canyon side would be blasted away and how much devastation would be caused.

With seemingly nothing to interfere with the burning fuse, he backed away and started to run across the open ground in the direction of the girl. He was about half way across when a man rose up from the ground and trained a gun on him.

'Hold it right there, stranger! I figure you had some part in this devastation, an' I'm goin' to see you get yours! My name is Frenchy Lafitte. I'd like you to know that for what time is left to you, because you're one who for sure won't see the next dawn!'

Chris slowly straightened up. He had felt for a long time that his luck was too good to last. He released his Winchester with some reluctance and awaited the inevitable brief flame from Lafitte's rifle muzzle. Before it could happen, however, there was a tremendous sheet of orange and yellow flame against the far cliff.

The whole of the canyon, including the soil on which they stood, appeared to shudder and shake. Rocks and plants, blasted from the north wall of the canyon, began to fly upwards and outwards. Lafitte was distracted. As the first of the rocks began to crash down on the canyon floor round about them an unexpected gun sounded off.

Lafitte leapt as though he had been stung. As a second bullet ripped into his body, he went over backwards, yet another casualty in that night of colossal slaughter. Nerena came running haphazardly, having fired the bullets which cut him down, and stumbled into the arms of Chris who hugged her to him.

While they stood there, wondering if any of the flying rock bolts would hit them another diversion occurred. The unmistakable crash and rattle of

Lieutenant Stride's gatling gun came up the confined space of the tunnel. The men caught in there called out in anguish and fear, their voices being drowned by the sheer volume of the multi-barrelled repeating gun fired directly into their midst from the other end.

Chris heard it, and knowing the sound of old, knew what it meant. The gun had been stripped down from its earlier point of devastation and somehow negotiated over the formidable stream which lacked a bridge. Stride, Bart and the smaller cavalry detail were actually coming in via the tunnel.

Upwards of a score of men died quickly in that tunnel. Still more backed out in haste, anxious to save their skins at any cost. Unfortunately for them, their retreat was ill-timed. A second sheet of yellow flame tinged with red erupted up the side of the canyon closest to them. The *arroyo* up which they were retreating vibrated frighteningly beneath their boots and for a time no one knew what to make of the phenomenon.

Almost as many again lost their lives in the explosions which the old Colonel had long since thought of as a defensive measure against outsiders. Once again huge flying lumps of rock, and whole boulders flew across the smoke-laden air within the canyon and the floor was littered more thickly than ever.

So pressing was the danger that Chris turned and ran back to the hacienda, taking Nerena by the hand. Not far beyond the shattered mouth of the canyon a cavalry bugle sounded, hinting that mounted men were about to launch an attack in the lull after cannon fire.

There was another burst from the gatling in the tunnel and then that went silent for good. After that, the gun-fire was limited to rifles and revolvers. Within half an hour, the handful of survivors who were seeking to deny the army access to the stronghold, fell back.

It was not clear where they were

retreating to and their withdrawal coincided with the arrival of a score of men on foot and on horseback from the tunnel. All the latest comers were in the uniform of the U.S. cavalry. Caught as they were by superior numbers coming from two directions, the remnant of Clervaux's one-time élite garrison threw down their arms.

From the turret viewing point, it was clear to Chris and Nerena that the troop from the tunnel led by a young officer with a torch and a drawn sword were now in control of the canyon floor.

'Those boys from the fort sure know how to go into action, Nerena, an' that's promisin'!' Chris remarked with enthusiasm.

Nerena looked up into his drawn face and saw the animation there. It was plain to her that he was a man of action, even if he had left the cavalry of his own free will.

'It seems strange to think of you as havin' no connection with the army,' she remarked lightly. 'Are there any circumstances under which you would join up again?'

Chris grinned and squeezed her arm. 'Well, if they made it attractive enough, I might jest rejoin. They'd have to make me an officer, of course, an' offer me married quarters for a wife. Always supposin' the right girl was keen on marryin' me in the first place.'

Nerena knew full well what was behind his remarks. She turned and draped her arms round his neck, drawing his head down to hers. They were still in the same embrace when a fair-haired corporal on a big chestnut horse came riding up with a torch in his hand for a closer look at the building.

The two in the turret both recognised him when he had still some way to come. They waved to him briefly and then ignored his approach for a while longer.

Other titles in the
Linford Western Library:

THE CHISELLER

Tex Larrigan

Soon the paddle-steamer would be on its long journey down the Missouri River to St Louis. Now, all Saul Rhymer had to do was to play the last master-stroke of the evening. He looked at the mounting pile of gold and dollar bills and again at the cards in his hand. Then, looking around the table, he produced the deed to the goldmine in Montana. 'Let's play poker!' But little did he know how that journey back to St Louis would change his life so drastically.